Dry Clean Only

by
Suzanne Sharma

authorHOUSE®

AuthorHouse™
1663 Liberty Drive, Suite 200
Bloomington, IN 47403
www.authorhouse.com
Phone: 1-800-839-8640

First published by AuthorHouse 3/31/2008

ISBN: 978-1-4343-4835-7 (sc)

Printed in the United States of America
Bloomington, Indiana

This book is printed on acid-free paper.

Cover design by Sajeevan Eswarakumar, 2xclusiv Enterprise.

Acknowledgements

There are so many people who have contributed to this book, many of them unknowingly.

First and foremost I would like to thank God for giving me the courage to pursue my dreams.

To Mom and Dad for their endless love and support. You taught me how to dream and I just hope to make you proud. To my sisters, Sheryl and Chrissy, for always being there for me. You have seen me through the good and bad times, and never left my side. I love you all very much.

To my friends for providing me with inspiration and material for much of this book. To Sala a.k.a. Vik for listening to me day after day as I strived to complete the story. I owe you the title! To Nidhi, Ken, Amo, Misha, Manik, Kaka, Pavan, Aman, Amardeep, Ravi, and Sean, for their constant encouragement and never letting me give up. Most importantly, I thank my C-Crew, Priya, Preet, Vandeep, Farrah, and Kim. I love you girls and honestly don't know where I'd be without you.

To my publisher, Anthony, for his patience and for always being available to answer my hundreds of questions, and to everyone else at AuthorHouse who assisted me along the way.

Also, a special thanks to everyone who actually picked up this book and intends to read it. You've given a girl who loves to write an outlet to her thoughts. I couldn't appreciate you more for this.

"Anything's possible if you've got enough nerve."

–J.K. Rowling

Prologue:

A Baffled Young Girl

Personality Test

1. What is your name?
   Jackie Malhotra
2. Are you male or female?
   Female
3. How old are you?
   22.........24
4. Do you prefer chocolate or candy?
   Chocolate
5. What is your favourite colour?
   At the moment, purple
6. What do you enjoy doing?
   Shopping, watching movies, partying,
   anything that doesn't involve too much work!
7. What is your occupation?
   Psychology major...
   Student teacher...
   Artist...
   Truthfully, I am in between jobs right now

Okay, I give up. What sort of personality test has to ask you such invasive questions? They should stick to simple yes/no type ones like 'Do you enjoy pizza?' where I could easily respond 'yes'. Oh forget it, these tests are such a scam anyway. How can they honestly tell me what type of person I am? The only person who truly knows me is me, and I know who I am. I enjoy great conversation, candlelit dinners, long walks on the beach…this is starting to sound like a dating resume.

Seriously though, it's not like I don't know what I want to do. It's just that there are so many options. And in order to do anything, I'd have to complete like four years of school! How can people really expect to go to school for every single profession? I thought about becoming a teacher, so I majored in English and then realised that after getting my B.A., I'd have to go to teacher's college for at least another year. So that idea was out the door. Then there was the time that I wanted to become an actress and I attended all of these courses through an agency, only to realise that I couldn't act to save my life. And ever since I was a child I've always wanted to become a veterinarian, but then I thought about all of those sick pets and I got too depressed.

Maybe it's just me. Most of my friends have gone to school, stuck with what they started studying and even have fulltime jobs right now. Except for Teresa, who is currently unemployed, lives at home with her parents, and whose sole ambition in life is to marry rich. Maybe that's one of the reasons she's been my best friend since we were sixteen. She's the only other person I know who's as lost as I am.

Wait, I didn't mean that. Of course I'm not lost or anything. It's just taking me longer to figure out how I'm going to accomplish all of the things that I want to do. But I know it won't be too much longer. It's just a matter of prioritizing really. I mean when you look at it, it's almost as simple as answering a yes or no question.

Part 1:

All Good Things Must Come To An End

"Janaki!"

Oh damn, I'd completely forgotten that I was supposed to go and pick up my mom from work. Now I can hear my dad yelling at me and he's not sounding too happy. It's never good when he uses my full name.

"Consider me already out the door," I say as I waltz by him.

"You know that you should leave half hour before?" he says sternly in his East Indian accent.

"Yes, I'm sorry. I was applying to some colleges," I lie easily.

"It better be application for the law school," he says with a nod of his head.

"I know," I say with a hint of irritation. "Dad, mom's gonna be standing outside waiting for me."

"Okay, go *beta*," he finally says, using his pet name for me.

I do not understand my parents' obsession with me becoming a lawyer. Ever since I can remember, they've pushed me towards that career path. And every time I tell them that I want to do something else, I can see the disappointment on their faces. They were ecstatic the day my evil cousin, Sonia, became a lawyer. And you know what the worst part is? She's a lawyer that deals with traffic tickets! She's not even in like criminal law or anything. This whole lawyer obsession must be an East Indian thing. If you don't go into law, medicine or business, then your parents think you're a complete failure.

As I pull into my mom's workplace, one thing is clear. She is really pissed off at the fact that I'm late. If there's one person who knows how to make me feel bad about something, it's my mom. I brace myself as she opens the car door.

"Hi mom," I say casually.

"You are late," she says stiffly.

"I know. I'm sorry. It won't happen again," I respond.

"This thing I've heard before," she retorts.

"Yeah, but mom, I was applying to colleges on the Internet, and I just had to finish up this one before I left," I lie. The way I see it, I've already lied, so why stop now?

"Don't lie to me," my mom says, her accent making her sound more threatening than usual. Shoot, I'd forgotten that she can always tell when I lie.

"Okay, you're right," I say in defeat. "I forgot to leave on time. But I really do feel bad about it. I'm sorry."

My mom's eyes finally soften. "I just don't know where your head is Janaki. We don't expect too much from you, I think. Just that you get a good job, find a good husband, and in meantime you have few responsibilities."

"I know," I say. When she gets like this, it's easier to agree with her than argue.

"I'm not your enemy," she says as we pull into the driveway. "I only want what is best for you."

That's the thing about parents. They always claim they want what is best for you. However, they also assume that they are the only ones who know what is best. My parents, for example, apart from wanting me to become a big shot lawyer, also want to make sure that I marry well. They expect me to marry someone of the same religion, social and financial status, and of course someone who is good looking. As if I don't have enough to worry about! Whatever happened to finding someone who treats me well, or makes me laugh, or someone who I love? Apparently none of that matters as much as how big his bank account is, or whether he goes to the same *Mandir* as me. I should really blow them away one day and tell them that I refuse to get married at all, or that I'm a lesbian or something. On second thought, I better not. I don't think I want to give either of them a heart attack.

University Application
Short Answer Questions:

1. Describe a moment that changed your life and the significance of that moment.
   When I was twelve, I was walking home from school one day and I saw an old woman in a wheelchair. She was sitting on her porch, talking to herself. At that second, I realised the importance of life. Here was this woman, who was old, senile and disabled. All I could hope for was that she'd lived her life to its fullest, because before you know it, it passes you by.

2. Who is someone that motivates you and why?
   My mother motivates me. She is always full of advice and encouragement. Even when I have no idea where I'm going or what I'm doing, all I have to do is talk to her and it gives me hope.

3. If there is one thing that you could change about yourself, what would it be and why?
   I would make myself less uptight and more relaxed. Sometimes, I think that I'm too much of a hard worker and perfectionist. While I have found this to be rewarding, I do sometimes find myself not having enough free time for myself.

Okay, so most of my answers have been exaggerated to make me sound more like a model student. So what if the old woman in the wheelchair is actually my next-door neighbour, crazy old Mrs. Norman, whom I see every single day? Maybe I don't actually reflect upon the importance of life when I see her, and instead just feel sorry for her and carry on my way. But it is true that my mother motivates me, even if when she does it, I get annoyed and tune her out. Question three was a complete joke though. Why would I want to change anything about myself? I mean, okay I'm not saying I'm perfect. But I think my flaws add character, so why change them? Personally, I think that that question was a trick question. They just want people to doubt themselves. It's probably a way for the admissions people to get rid of the losers and only accept people who are strong and confident. In fact, I think I should change my answer and let them know that I know what they're up to.

I wake up to the sound of the alarm on Tuesday morning and immediately hit the snooze button. I don't really know why my mom insists that I set it. It's not like I need to get up at 8:30am to do anything. At the moment, I'm not in school, and I don't have a job, so what's the point of waking up early? But every time I tell her this, she just shakes her head and says she refuses to have a lazy daughter.

By noontime, I finally decide that I've watched enough TV and eaten enough cereal. I think it's about time for me to give Teresa a call since she should be awake by now. Her parents let her sleep in as late as she wants!

"Hello," I hear Teresa's groggy voice answer.

"Hey babe! What's the plan for today?" I ask.

"What time is it?" she asks, ignoring my question.

"It's just past noon and I'm super bored," I respond. "So let's hit up the mall or something."

"Okay, give me an hour to get ready," she says, still sounding half asleep.

"Deal," I answer enthusiastically.

This is one of the things I love about Teresa. She's up for anything at anytime. I could call her on a random Wednesday night at 2am and tell her that I can't sleep and that I'm coming over for a drink. By the time I got to her place, she'd be waiting with martinis. In fact, I'm pretty sure I've done something like that on a few occasions. I remember this one time that my car got a flat tire at like 7:30am, while I was on my way to one of my part-time jobs. I called her and she arrived at the scene within fifteen minutes, with her then boyfriend, carrying a spare tire and a jack. Of course she wasn't able to fix the flat on her own, but she brought with her someone who could and that's what really matters. I wish there were more people like Teresa in this world.

I feel like people would be less depressed if they had a friend like her who would always be there when you needed them.

Two hours later, at the mall, we've only just begun to shop. We're at one of my favourite stores, Bebe. Okay, I know the prices are a little extreme, but the quality is really good. Except for that one shirt I bought, which ripped after the second time I wore it. But honestly, I bought it on sale so I can't really expect much, can I?

I'm trying on a pair of jeans in a size 26 waist, even though I really need a 28. The way I see it though, if I buy one size smaller, it'll motivate me to lose the extra couple inches. I'm just squeezing into them, when I hear a gasp from outside my change room.

"What is it Teresa?" I call.

"You have to come and see who's here," she whispers.

My curiosity gets the best of me and I give up trying to put on the too small jeans. I throw on my own pair and step out of the fitting room.

Damn, standing only twenty feet away is Danny, my ex-boyfriend. The last time I saw him was about four months ago. I left him in the middle of an empty parking lot and drove away. Trust me, the idiot totally deserved it.

"Walk by him and act like you don't know him," suggests Teresa.

"I can't do that," I exclaim. "I've got to be mature about this."

"Okay, so go and talk to him," she continues.

"No way, why would I want to acknowledge a weirdo like him?" I say.

"Too late, he's coming this way," she whispers while walking away.

As he gets closer, I look up. He's definitely looking better than I remember. He looks like he's been working out, which is strange because I would always try to get him to tone up his slim frame, but he would refuse. And wait a second, did he get contacts? And he's not wearing his usual baseball cap and jeans. He's dressed in a sophisticated polo shirt and khakis.

"Hi Jackie," he says casually.

"Hi Danny," I say nonchalantly. "You look different."

"Yeah, my new girlfriend, Crystal, does bring out the best in me."

New girlfriend? Well that explains it. He's trying to make me jealous. Too bad, I couldn't care less. The poor guy never was that smart. That was one of his biggest flaws. He could never understand me, especially towards the end of our relationship.

"Aw, that's nice," I say, sweetly. "Hopefully she can put up with your bitching and whining longer than I could."

I flip my hair and turn to walk away, leaving him totally speechless.

When you first take a look at Danny Kapoor, he seems to have quite a lot going for him. He's what I'd call a good on paper sort of guy. He's rich, attractive, comes from a good family, etc. I was instantly interested in him when I met him at District, a local club. He bought me drinks the whole night, danced with me like a gentleman, which means no bumping and grinding, and he even introduced me to his friends as, "This amazing woman he couldn't believe he'd just met." The first two weeks of our relationship passed by with me thinking that this could go somewhere. But like everything that seems too good to be true, it was.

Enter psycho Danny, which is what I'd started to call him in my mind. He became possessive, annoying, and practically violent. He would call me ten times a day to see where I was, then show up to see if I'd been telling the truth. He didn't like me having any male friends, and would even get jealous if I told him I was spending the night out with Teresa. Eventually, after about three months of this, I got sick of it and told him that it was over. This is when the real psycho revealed himself. Danny threatened to hurt himself if I ever left him. Luckily, I knew him well enough to know he was bluffing. Danny might be a lot of things, but wimp and loser topped the list. I never believed he would actually have the balls to go through with it. Thank God I was right.

Who is your Soul Mate?

1. Do you prefer men or women?
   Men

2. What is your ideal date?
   Definitely something more fun than the typical movie and dinner deal. Anything that involves a great conversation, the man pays, and I can wear my little black dress.

3. At what age would you like to be married by?
   Sometime before I start to sag. Everyone knows it's all down hill from there.

4. Describe your perfect wedding party.
   Lots of people, maybe on the beach, champagne, very romantic setting

5. How many children do you plan on having?
   Children? Can we please get through the dating ritual before we even start to think about kids?

Results:

Based on your answers, you aren't looking for something that is necessarily long-term and could enjoy a fling. Your perfect match would be someone who is strong, and very talkative.

You would do well to find someone who is easy-going and who enjoys compromise. Love Match: Pisces, Scorpio. Lucky Days for Romance: 10, 15, 24.

About two weeks ago I printed out an online quiz and had to mail in my answers. Then I waited for what seemed like forever for them to mail me back my results and this is what they sent me? Wow, that was a complete waste of time. The quiz basically told me that I'm promiscuous and controlling and that I should find someone who'll sit quietly and take my crap. Like I didn't already know that.

Fridays are the best day by far because they're the start of the weekend. Tonight I've got plans with Teresa to go and hit a bar in the city. We'll probably end up drinking too much, talking to random guys and by the end of the night at Denny's, which is an after partying must. It's just about the only 24-hour restaurant that serves breakfast all day. Where else can you get French toast at 4am?

I make my way down the stairs at around 11am, and immediately know that I'm in big trouble. My parents are both sitting at the kitchen table looking very pissed. I assume it must be because I've slept in. Maybe it's because I forgot to clean my room, or the fact that I was up late last night on the phone. Oh no, please don't let them have overheard me talking to Teresa about how many guys we were going to pick up tonight.

"Janaki, there was a letter in the mail for you," starts dad.

"Oh really?" I say cautiously.

"Yes, you would like to explain yourself?" asks mom.

"Um, well could you be a little bit more specific?" I ask hopefully.

"It is from University of Toronto," offers mom.

I relax for a minute. This can't possibly be as bad as I'd thought. Even if they rejected my application, I've still got tons of options.

"Your application was denied, and your mother and I have had it up to here." dad says holding his hand above his head.

Okay, this might be slightly worse than I'd thought, especially now that I can see the vein in dad's neck popping out.

"I'm sorry *beta*, but it is time for something serious, and we think there is only one way," dad continues.

"You must move out," mom says gravely.

"WHAT?" I exclaim. "You're kicking me out?"

"You leave no choice," dad says, shaking his head.

"How can you do this to your only daughter?" I shriek dramatically.

"We think it is time for you to stand on your own two feet," mom says. "We give you too many chances and you never provide us with the results."

"So you're throwing me out of the house?" I say shrilly. "How do you expect me to survive without a job?"

"Then you get a job," dad says suddenly. "Listen *beta*, it will be good for you. It will give you the chance to be responsible. We can see that schooling is not something that interests you. So, if no school, then time for work."

"Yeah, but do you know what sort of job I'm going to get without any degree?" I cry. "Nothing!"

"I do not have a degree," says mom. "I came from India only doing tenth grade. I married your Papa and was a housewife for fifteen years before getting a job."

"So you expect me to work in some warehouse for pennies like you did?" I say, my anger getting the best of me.

"Do not disrespect your mother!" shouts dad, and I immediately regret what I said. Still, the injustice of it all makes me fume.

"You had each other," I continue, lowering my voice slightly. "And you're sending me off completely on my own."

"You're saying you would like us to find you a good husband then?" says mom, almost hopefully.

"This is ridiculous!" I say. "Of course not, I'm just pointing out that you two came here together for a better life and had each other for support. If you kick me out, I'll have no one!"

"Janaki, that is where you are wrong," says mom. "You will always have us. But we think there is no other choice. This change will help you be mature and responsible. Trust us, we know what is best."

There it is again, they know what's best. If I had a nickel for every time they said that, I'd actually be able to afford my own condo. Unfortunately, as it stands, I'm screwed. I've already scanned some of the newspapers and who knew that rent was so expensive? My parents have offered to pay my first and last month, but that still leaves me with all the months in between! I honestly can't believe that they expect me to move out. It's totally against East Indian custom to throw an unmarried, uneducated girl out on her own. However, according to them, my priority right now is to find a job. And I'm not allowed to do anything else until then. No partying, no going to the mall with Teresa since my credit cards have been taken away from me, nothing. Right now I'm either job hunting or apartment hunting, which means I'm allowed to go online or read the paper. Great, there goes my Friday night.

Classifieds

Looking for a roommate.
One bedroom condo, one bath, 5 appliances, no pets, must be able to dance.
$700+utilities

Studio apartment, one and a half bath, no appliances, near subway and airport, available next year.
$900+utilities

Immediate opening
1 bedroom basement, one and a half bath, 5
appliances, no smoking, no drinking, no pets,
no parties
$700 inclusive

What is wrong with the world? Every time I read an ad and think that this could be a good one, I get towards the end and realise that people are really messed up. What kind of a sick, perverted person would put that it's a requirement for their roommate to be able to dance? And how can anyone insist that there will be no parties, smoking, drinking, etc. in their basement when the person will be paying them rent? I'm getting so annoyed. This looks like it's going to be much harder than I thought.

That evening, my head feels as if it's going to burst from stress. I can't believe that I had to call and cancel on Teresa. I don't even remember the last time I cancelled on her. I'm considering what I should do with myself for the rest of the night since I can't bring myself to look at another ad, when I hear a knock on my main floor bedroom window.

"Teresa," I say in surprise. I can see her blonde head looking at me, a huge grin on her face.

I run over to open the window. "What are you doing here?"

"I came to rescue you," she says hurriedly. "Quick, get dressed and let's go."

"Are you crazy? I can't sneak out of my house. I'm too old for that!" I exclaim.

"Yeah," she continues, "that's the best part. It'll rejuvenate us."

I consider my options. I could sit at home all night, bored out of my mind. Or go and have some fun with my girl. I mean I don't really have a choice when you look at it. And technically I was supposed to be going out tonight anyway.

"Okay, I'm in," I say quickly. "Give me ten minutes to get ready."

"Don't forget the plan," she whispers before ducking out of sight.

The plan! I'd almost forgotten. When we were much younger, the two of us came up with a strategy to sneak out of the house. This is way up and above the typical 'stuff pillows under your blanket to make it look like you're sleeping' routine. See, the problem with that idea is that your parents could easily come in, take the blankets off and realise that you've snuck out. Our plan is fairly simple actually. All it involves is some carefully crafted dialogue with my parents.

"Mom, Dad," I call as I enter the living room. The two of them are watching an old Indian movie starring Shahrukh Khan, who has got to be one of the most gorgeous and talented actors ever.

"Yes," they say in unison.

"Look, maybe I was a bit harsh before," I start. "I understand why the two of you are suggesting that I move out. And honestly, don't worry about me. It's about time that I grow up."

I can see the touched expressions on their faces and know that phase one is going well. It's time to kick into phase two.

"Anyway, I've been searching through the papers all day and am really tired, so I think it's best for me to get some sleep," I say at last.

"Of course *beta*," says dad. "We'll turn down the volume. You go sleep and we will talk more tomorrow."

"Goodnight," I say, trying to hide the excitement from my voice.

Works like a charm every time. I know my parents well enough to know they wouldn't dare disturb me for the rest of the night. Who needs to stuff pillows under a blanket when you have your parents trust?

Much later that night, I've had too much to drink and am staring into the face of a complete stranger. Teresa is right beside me, ordering another round.

"Whatdya say your name was again?" Mr. Alcohol asks me, slurring his words slightly.

"I didn't," I respond casually. He could be cute if he wasn't so drunk.

"Jackie," Teresa calls, handing me a drink.

"Jackiiiieee," Mr. Alcohol says triumphantly as I roll my eyes.

Teresa looks at me and laughs. I immediately know she's up to no good. She casually throws her arm around my shoulder and turns to face Mr. Alcohol.

"Are you bothering my twin sister?" she asks accusingly.

Mr. Alcohol looks from her to me in bewilderment. There is no way that anyone could confuse Teresa and me for twins. I'm East Indian and she's Caucasian! However, Mr. Alcohol is obviously intoxicated so this should be fun.

"No, sis, he was just asking me for my name," I say innocently.

"You guys aren't twins," he says stupidly.

"Well, not identical of course," I say as if he's just said the most ridiculous thing.

"Yeah, but, but," he stammers. "You're not white!"

"Our dad was white, and mom was brown," says Teresa. "When mom had twins, one of us went on our dad's side and one on mom's."

"Really?" asks Mr. Alcohol.

God, people can be so lame. I can't believe he's actually buying this garbage.

"Well yeah," I say. "Why would we lie about it?"

"Wow, that's incredible," he says finally. "You should be on TV or something!"

"That's a great idea!" exclaims Teresa. "But you know, once we're famous, we won't be able to talk to just anyone at a bar."

"Yeah…" he trails off.

"Yeah, especially guys who wear blue shirts," I say, noticing his attire.

"And guys who drink gin and tonic," Teresa says, nodding at his drink.

Mr. Alcohol finally gets the hint. "Oh, okay, well you twins have fun then," he says, wandering off.

The second he's gone, Teresa and I burst out laughing. We've done the twin bit so many times before, yet it never seems to get old.

Men are so much more simple minded than women. I once heard that the way to a man's heart is through his stomach, and I can definitely vouch for that. During my short-lived relationship with Kam, an obsessive-compulsive student teacher, I learned that all I had to do was bring him food and I could have my heart's desire. I once asked him for one hundred dollars over a plate of spaghetti, and he didn't even look up while tossing me his wallet. If it was the other way around and a guy had asked his girlfriend for that sort of money, she probably would've asked him a million questions until the guy finally gave up. This is probably one of the many reasons I could never date a woman; they're too uptight.

The following morning, I wake up with a splitting headache and I promise myself that I will never drink again. It's funny how many times I have vowed just that, and yet the next time liquor is involved, I'm the first one ordering drinks.

I can hear my mom banging on my door, and telling me that I have twenty minutes to get ready. All I want to do is curl up and hide under the covers. What is she talking about anyway? Get ready for what? And then it hits me. It's my little cousin's birthday today, and I completely forgot to get her a gift. Nalini is going to kill me! The 12-year old girl totally looks up to me, her older and wiser cousin. And I'd promised her that I'd get her that new Hilary Duff CD.

I jump out of bed and wonder what I can do to rectify the situation. I have no time to make a quick stop at the mall, considering that the party starts soon and my family has to be there extra early to help cook and decorate. I realise that I have two choices. I can either 'fess up and hope that she doesn't hate me forever, or I can tell a small white lie and tell her that her present is on its way or something. Obviously, I'll have to do the latter. I mean it really is for Nalini's own good. Her heart would probably break if she knew the horrible truth.

I ignore the pounding in my head and shower and change as quickly as possible. I have to wear an Indian suit. So far that's the only good part of the whole situation. I rarely ever get to wear my Indian clothes, and I have so many beautiful outfits that Nani, my grandmother, sent me from India. I'm putting on my *bindi* when my mom shouts that she and dad are leaving this minute, with or without me. I decide to apply my lipstick in the car to save time. It's bad enough that I forgot Nalini's gift, it'll be even worse if I don't show up at all.

The car ride over is quite a bore. Mom and dad ask me if I've had any luck with my job or apartment hunting and I quickly answer no. They both give me a disapproving look and continue on in silence.

We arrive at the party an hour and a half late, which isn't bad considering that we're still practically the first ones to arrive. Most East Indian people run on a completely different schedule than everyone else in the world. We call it Indian Standard Time, which means that it's customary to arrive approximately two hours later than the invitation time.

My mom disappears into the kitchen with all the other women to help cook, and my dad saunters over to the living room where all the men are sitting and enjoying a game of cards. I scan the rooms until I spot Nalini sitting with all of her friends. She shrieks, runs towards me and throws her skinny arms around me in a surprisingly tight hug, which I return.

Nalini then asks me if I was able to get her the Hilary Duff CD. What is it with kids? They have absolutely no patience. I look down into her expectant face, shake my head no and I can immediately see the disappointment in her eyes.

"Wait, no this is good," I say, trying to salvage the situation.

"How?" asks Nalini suspiciously.

"Because, what I got you is so much better!" I say enthusiastically.

"Really?" Nalini says hopefully. "What did you get me Jackie?"

"Well…" I trail off. Damn, I wasn't quite prepared for this question yet. "I am going to take you to the mall to buy you whatever you want!"

"Wow," exclaims Nalini. "This is better than a CD. I get to go to the mall with you and buy a present!"

"Exactly," I say triumphantly. Whew, thank God I'm good at thinking on the spur of the moment. Now let's just hope that what she picks out isn't like a Prada purse or something. I definitely don't have the funds for that right now.

And just as I'm getting out of that sticky situation, I see another one approaching me. About ten feet away and getting closer by the second is evil cousin Sonia.

"Hi Jackie," she says in her snotty voice. "So nice of you to get off your throne and show up."

I check to make sure that Nalini has left before I continue. I do not want her to hear this exchange. Although she knows that Sonia and I don't get along, the last thing I want is to have her actually witness it.

"Of course, I wouldn't miss Nalini's birthday for the world," I say casually. "It's just too bad that you had to be here as well."

"Well, since I am Nalini's favourite cousin..." Sonia says matter-of-factly.

I laugh at the thought. "In your dreams Sonia."

"Oh please, don't tell me that you honestly believe that she'd chose you over me," says Sonia.

"Yeah, it's a tough choice," I start. "I mean, I'm nice to her and enjoy spending time with her. And you are boring, stuck up and only want her to like you so that you can hold it against me."

"That's not true!" Sonia gasps.

"Don't kid yourself," I say with an air of haughtiness.

"I'm not," says Sonia. "Why would she choose you, a dead beat loser who hasn't worked in like a year and can't get into a college, over me, a successful lawyer who is also in a serious relationship."

I stare back for a second at a loss for words. I've heard her say things like that before, but it still gets to me every time. The girl knows exactly what buttons to push.

"Simple," I say, regaining my confidence. "Because I'm more fun." And with that, I turn and walk away, leaving Sonia scowling after me.

Sonia and I used to get along perfectly. From the age of seven to fourteen, I almost never left her side. I used to look up to her as the big sister I never had since she's almost four years older. She would come over and we'd have a tea party, and play with our dolls. I mean, she even taught me how to apply make up and talked me through my first crush. It's funny how things change. I remember the exact day everything became different. His name was Manny and he went to school with Sonia. They were acquaintances, meaning that they'd say hello in the halls, but it never emerged into anything more. I was supposed to meet her after her class one day, and bumped into Manny. I immediately fell for him. He was so not your typical East Indian boy. He looked more like he was Spanish, if anything. I can still remember his wavy brown hair and green eyes. Green eyes, seriously! We started to talk and flirt, and he even asked me if I had plans for Friday night. Then Sonia came out of her class, caught the exchange and I could see I'd done something wrong. How was I to know that she had had a crush on Manny since the beginning of the semester? You'd think that the two of us being as close as we were, she'd have told me. But that was it, because after that day, Sonia refused to forgive me and accused me of always trying to put her down. Sometimes I think that men could be the cause of all evil.

A few hours into the party, I'm munching on a *samosa* when Bindu Auntie reaches over and gives my shoulder a sympathetic squeeze. I look at her, wondering what this is all about.

"Hi Auntie," I say. "How are you?"

In our culture, every adult automatically becomes your Uncle or Auntie, regardless of whether they're actually related to you or not. Bindu Auntie is actually one of the women that Nalini's mother works with.

"I have just heard the news," Bindu Auntie starts. "It's terrible that your parents are wanting you to move out."

I look at her, a little surprised. I didn't expect my society conscious parents to tell anyone that they'd kicked me, their only child, out of the house. It would probably ruin their reputation.

"Uh, yeah," I start. "It's not so bad though. It's about time that I started my own life." The last thing I want is to make this into a bigger deal than it already is.

"Yes, but what will you do?" asks Bindu Auntie dramatically. "Where will you go?"

"I'll be fine," I reassure her, wondering why I'm the one doing the reassuring. Someone should be comforting me through this traumatic event.

"But it is a very rough world outside," she presses.

I've had enough of this. I need to find my parents and ask them how they could tell the whole world that they've thrown me out on my own.

"Auntie, don't worry. I have you to fall back on if anything," I say. The best way out of a conversation with a relative is to make them feel wanted and then make a quick exit.

"Of course Janaki," she beams. "My doors are always open for you."

I quickly hug her and then rush off to find mom and dad. I see them both almost immediately. They're standing in a corner, eating food out of one plate. It really grosses me out to see my parent's act fondly with each other in any sort of way.

"So, you thought you'd let everyone know that I've been thrown out of the house?" I ask rudely.

"What? Who knows?" my mom asks, and from the look on her face I can tell that she hasn't told anyone.

"Bindu Auntie just came up to me and questioned me about it." I respond.

"But how could she know?" asks mom, looking around. "We wouldn't dare to tell anyone. It will make us look bad."

This response makes me slightly angry. Mom seems more worried about her reputation than the fact that her daughter will be leaving her house forever.

"Well, she knows!" I say in a shrill voice.

Mom turns to dad, and I can automatically see the guilty look on his face. Great, now there's going to be a fight.

"Who did you tell?" asks mom.

"Only Suresh," says dad defensively.

"Suresh!" my mom hisses. "You know that man cannot keep his mouth shut."

"Prabha," my dad says to mom. "He is my brother. And I will not have you talking badly about a member of my family."

Mom pouts, but doesn't answer.

"All I told him was that Janaki will be living on her own," dad reassures.

"You could very well have told him that we're kicking her out and disowning her," mom whispers dramatically.

"Which you practically are," I put in, knowing that as soon as the words are out of my mouth, I shouldn't have said them. Damn, now mom's anger is directed towards me.

"Janaki, we have discussed this before," says mom. "And what happened to the good girl from last night? You said you understood the decision."

Shoot, now I'm really screwed. I totally forgot about my con from last night.

"Well, maybe I changed my mind," I answer weakly.

Lucky for me mom turns back to dad and lashes out. "See what you've done now? You tell Suresh, now Bindu knows and she has filled Janaki's head with the garbage."

Wow, I totally didn't see that turning out like that. However, there's a bigger problem at hand. Because of mom's outburst, our little family argument has attracted a few people's attention. Conversations from nearby have halted and I can see many ears perking up to listen to us. It strikes me again just how nosy my relatives can be.

"Look, mom, dad," I whisper, turning to them both. "Let's continue this at home. We don't need to put on a show for everyone."

"Good idea," dad says with a grateful smile.

Unfortunately that's not the last that I hear of my dilemma. Before the end of the party, everyone knows. Sonia gleefully takes every chance she gets to rub it in. She even tells me that I'm such a disappointment that my parents gave up on me. But as bad as that sounds, it's not my main concern. I feel horrible for Nalini. She should be in the spotlight, and instead, her birthday has been ruined because of me. I make a mental note to buy her a Prada purse if that's what she really wants, even if it means taking out a loan from the bank.

Classifieds

We are looking for a team player to join our growing company. Must be very outgoing, enthusiastic and work well under pressure. We require candidates to have at least five years experience in sales. Please e-mail resumes to chantelle@travelsales.com

Are you looking for a new and exciting career that pays well? Do you prefer working minimal hours from the comfort of your own home?

Have you always dreamed of a career that could make you famous? This could be the perfect job for you! Pay can be as high as 1500/week. For more information call 416-555-5555.

Painter needed! Hours of work are Tues-Sat 12:00pm-7:00pm. Pay starts at $7/hour. No experience required! All interested applicants should call Tracey at 647-555-5555.

Okay, so any job that I have the training for either doesn't pay well, has weird hours or both. How am I supposed to find a job where I'll be able to afford an apartment? I've done the math and it looks like I'll be thrown out on the streets by the fourth month for sure. There's no way that I'll be able to work, pay my rent, bills, and take care of miscellaneous expenses. But I guess I don't have much choice. I'll have to suck it up and deal with it because my mom told me that I've only got a few weeks before she expects me out. Maybe if I at least try to live on my own, and fail, my parents will realise that they've made a mistake and take me back under their roof. Yeah, I think at this point, that's my best hope. Why does it seem like the second ad is looking for a porn star?

That night, as I'm applying a final coat of mascara, I hear my cell phone ring. It's Teresa of course.
"Hello," I answer.

"Hey, I'll be there to pick you up in ten minutes. You better be ready," warns Teresa.

"Of course I'll be ready," I say defensively. "See you soon!"

"Bye," she calls as she hangs up.

I throw the phone down and scurry around my room, throwing on my tank top and skirt at lightening speed. Shoot, I still need to run the flat iron through my hair. She's going to kill me if I'm even a second late. It's not my fault that I was raised by parents who are always late.

Tonight we've got plans to hit up the newest hot spot in town, Devil's. It should be a great time because we're also going to be joined by our other two friends, Julie and Christian. Any night out with either of them is always memorable. We'll probably have some sort of a scene because Julie can get feisty when jerks try to dance with her and I'm sure I'll have to tear Christian away from some guy by the end of the night as he declares that this one could be 'the one'.

I met the two of them while I was working at Aldo three years ago. Christian was helping Julie pick a pair of stilettos that made her super long legs look even longer. The three of us started talking and the next thing I knew I was having drinks with them after my shift. I introduced them to Teresa later that week, and before long, we'd all become good friends. Christian even consoled me through a bad break-up with this guy, Dave, that I'd been seeing and I in return helped him realise that the fact that he was gay made him unique, not weird. Or maybe it was him that made me realise that as well.

Damn, my phone's ringing again and I don't even have to look at it to know that it's Teresa calling to tell me she's outside.

As I hurry down the stairs, I notice my parents must have worked out their disagreement from earlier today because they're cuddled together on the couch, watching yet another Indian movie. This time it's an oldie with Hema Malini, who was really talented at the time, but in my opinion she let herself go towards the end of her career. If she'd wanted, she could still have been a big name in Bollywood today.

"Mom, dad, I see you two are getting along just fine now," I say as I observe them.

"Yes, we have worked it out and as usual your father knows I was right," mom says smugly.

My dad rolls his eyes and shrugs. "People would have found out sooner or later."

"Well, thanks for letting me go out tonight," I call as I head towards the door.

I don't know how or why but they both agreed to let me go downtown tonight without any arguments. Normally I have to beg and coax them for a few hours before they give in. It's so annoying! Teresa once explained to me that they just do it because they care and worry about me, especially because I'll be coming home at like 4am. She said she wished her parents worried about her as much as mine worry about me. I think she has no idea what she's talking about.

Much later that night, the four of us are crowded around the bar, ordering another round of tequila shots. Personally, I hate tequila, but the shots are so much fun to do when you're in a group. I down the shot. It must be like my eighth but I can't be sure because a familiar warm, fuzzy feeling is starting to surround me which means I'm getting drunk.

I look up to see Julie flirting with the bartender, who looks strikingly like Paul Walker. I know she's probably trying to get free drinks. My assumption is correct when minutes later I see her take three shots in a row with him. Then she stumbles up to me and whispers in my ear.

"I'm going upstairs to the VIP room with the sexy bartender," she winks. "Watch Christian, okay?"

I nod. Yeah, it's just a typical night for us all. Half way through it, Julie disappears with some random guy, Christian is curiously looking around for someone to dance with, Teresa is talking animatedly with some people and I'm getting drunk and watching it all. I feel a tap on my shoulder and I look over to see Christian smiling at me.

"Hey, what's going on?" I ask.

"Not much. You having a good time?" he asks.

"Yeah, how about you?"

"Well, there's this guy in the corner over there," Christian points.

I look to see a fairly attractive guy standing by himself. He's wearing a slinky dress shirt and fitted jeans. He's sipping a sex on the beach.

"Definitely gay," I tell Christian.

"Well I already know that," Christian puts in. "And don't act like you can tell just because he's dressed well and is drinking something fruity."

"So sorry," I say with a laugh. "So go up to him then."

This is all the persuasion that Christian needs. He marches right up to the guy and buys him another drink. Within minutes they're laughing and fairly soon after they're even dancing together.

I find myself smiling. It's so hard for Christian to find someone he's interested in because he's probably the pickiest person in the world. I remember the last relationship he had was over a year ago with this older guy named Sam. It was one of the strangest relationships I've heard of to this day. Sam was a businessman who would travel all over the world. He would be gone for weeks at a time, but would faithfully call Christian everyday. He would even send him postcards or little gifts from wherever he happened to be at the time. Eventually we found out that Sam was a gigolo, but not your average gigolo. His area of expertise included meeting rich men on the Internet. These men would then send Sam a plane ticket, put him in a fancy hotel and give him sort of like an all expenses paid vacation. All Sam had to do was put out. You can imagine Christian's shock and hurt when he accidentally came across one of the e-mails from one of Sam's many men. Needless to say, no matter how much Sam apologized or told Christian that he loved him, their relationship came to an abrupt end.

I'm lost in thought when I feel another tap on my shoulder. This time it's a complete stranger, but a very handsome stranger.

"Can I buy you a drink?" he asks.

"I don't accept drinks from strangers," I say with a smile.

"Shawn Virdi," he introduces himself.

"Jackie Malhotra," I respond.

"Well now that we're not strangers, I suppose I can buy you a drink," he says.

"I've already got one," I say not missing a beat. I love playing hard to get.

"Well, I guess it's just not my lucky night," he says with a smirk. He reaches for my hand, kisses it and turns to walk away.

I watch him disappear into the crowd, thinking that maybe I've made a mistake. Then I realise that he's left his business card, complete with a phone number, in my hand.

The next morning I hear my alarm go off and I curse under my breath. I pop two aspirin in my mouth and drain the glass of water that I was smart enough to put on my nightstand before passing out last night. I shower and dress quickly. Then I breathe a huge sigh of relief as I feel the last of my hangover disappear. Every Sunday we go to the *Mandir* and I highly doubt that it's appropriate to show up at a place of worship with the remains of last nights' alcohol still in your bloodstream. My mom once heard that "A family that prays together stays together," and as long as I can remember, we've never missed a Sunday at the *Mandir*.

"Janaki!" yells mom. "We are leaving!"

"I'm coming," I call back to her.

I trip over my purse and its contents spill out. I see a familiar piece of paper and smile to myself. It says, "Shawn Virdi, Public Relations."

I stick his business card in my nightstand and decide to wait the typical three days before I give him a call. Waiting fewer days might seem desperate. And if I wait too long, he might forget who I am. Personally, I think whoever came up with the three-day rule is a genius.

A few hours later, after praying, the three of us are downstairs eating *prasad*. I don't know what it is about the food at the *Mandir*, but it always tastes amazing, plus it's served throughout all hours of the day.

"How are you doing with the searching?" asks dad between mouthfuls of *roti*.

"It's coming along," I say.

"You know, Bobby was mentioning that he might be able to find you a basement," mom says casually.

"What?" I hiss. "I can't believe you asked Bobby for help!"

Bobby is Sonia's boyfriend. Asking him for help is just as bad as asking the ice queen herself!

"Look *beta*," says dad calmly. "He called last night and offered. You don't have to take the help if you don't want to."

"I don't care who called who, dad," I answer. "I can manage on my own."

"Fine then," says mom. "When you are out on the streets with no job and no home, don't come back then, asking Bobby for help."

"Trust me, I won't," I answer coldly.

With that, the three of us go back to eating in silence.

Personally, I have no problem what so ever with Bobby. In fact, I think that he's a great guy and I can't believe that he settled for Sonia. The two of them met a little over a year ago and from what I've heard through the grapevine, they've finally told the family and are discussing marriage. From the sound of it, they'll probably be married before the end of next year. I just hope that I'm at least in a relationship by then. Not because I necessarily want a relationship, but just because I cannot stand the thought of Sonia gloating about how I'm still single and she's getting married. Actually, I change my mind. If I'm hoping for stuff, I hope that Bobby comes to his senses before then and realises that he's making a huge mistake.

To Jackie Malhotra:
We have received your application for the position of Customer Service Representative and regret to inform you that the position has been filled. However, we will keep your resume

on file for the next six months in case anything else opens up.

Sincerely,
Tim Jones
The Credit Union

To Jackie Malhotra:
Your resume has been received and we have had the chance to review it. Unfortunately, we find that you don't have the necessary qualifications for the position of Junior Vice President at our Toronto headquarters. If a position becomes available that you meet the requirements for, we will be sure to notify you.

Jeff Robbins
Human Resources
Fashion One

I know it's only been a few days, but I was really hoping that by now I might at least have scored an interview. Unfortunately all I've been getting are e-mails of rejection. I never thought that looking for a job could be so hard! From what I remember, half of the other times that I got one, I barely even had to apply. This one time I just walked into a store and they gave me a job after I talked a fellow customer into buying a top because the colour suited her. You know I honestly think that all jobs should be offered that way. Okay, so maybe many of my past jobs have been in retail, and the jobs that I've been applying to now are more fulltime office work, but I still think that it would simplify things if we could all just skip the whole interview process. You can really tell the most about a person within one minute of talking to them. Even the resume doesn't do a person justice. Maybe I should just start calling these businesses and demanding that they hire me. It would definitely show that I'm motivated. And then I could also tell them that they've been doing the hiring process wrong all these years. In fact, they should be so lucky to have an employee like me who could show them how to make things easier and save time.

It's Tuesday and I've been staring at the phone for the last ten minutes. I've dialled Shawn's number about five times and each time I've hung up. I don't know why I'm so nervous all of a sudden. I mean I talked to the guy for like a second three days ago. So what if he's just the most handsome man who's ever approached me and probably also the most successful? So what if I can't stop thinking about the way his deep voice dripped with confidence? None of it really matters. I mean, if it's meant to be, it's meant to be, right? I just need to suck it up, call him and stop acting like one of those nervous teenage girls who've never called a guy in their entire life. I've called plenty of guys before. I pick up the phone and dial his number before my nerves hit me again. It rings once, twice, three times then clicks to the answering machine. Shoot! I wasn't prepared to leave a message. I'm just trying to think of what I should say, when I hear the beep, which totally catches me off guard.

"Uh, hi Shawn," I squeak. I clear my throat and try again. "I hope you remember me. We um, met at Devil's a few nights ago. I was just calling to um, say that, ah, maybe it could be your lucky night now," I pause, noticing how stupid I sound.

The nerves get the best of me and I quickly hang up before I realise what I've done. Oh God, no. What have I done? I need to go back two minutes in time. Where is a time turner when you need one? He's going to hear that message and laugh. Then he'll never call me back again. What's even worse is that I think I ended it by making myself sound like one of those sex line operators. I'm cursing myself for being such a moron when it hits me that I didn't even leave my name, or a call back number. I hope he has call display. Then I shake my head. Well, after that message, I guess I really don't have to stress about whether or not he's going to call me back.

The end of the week arrives before I even realise it. Shawn still hasn't called me and I've decided to ship him off to the land of lost boys. It's a place where I like to retire old boyfriends, bad dates and losers in general. I don't know why I even expected him to call me back, but I guess there was a little hope left somewhere in the back of my head. However, now it's been three days and nothing. So I think it's safe to move on.

To make matters worse, I cannot believe I've spent the entire week scouting jobs and apartments with no luck. I haven't received a single call for an interview, and the apartment hunting is going terrible. I visited this one place, a two-bedroom basement apartment with full kitchen, bathroom, living room and a separate entrance. I really thought it would be amazing, until I actually entered it that is. It smelled like death mixed with a bit of garlic for an added kick. Needless to say, I was out of there before the owners realised I'd even entered.

I decide to put all of my worries aside for the moment as I pull up into Nalini's driveway. Today we decided to go shopping since I owe her a wonderful birthday present. She comes running down the driveway and jumps into my car, full of excitement.

"Hey sweetie, you ready to go shopping?" I ask.

"Yep," she exclaims.

"Great, because we've got a lot of ground to cover, and a lot of cash to spend," I say, thinking of the credit card I was able to persuade my dad to lend me for the day.

"I hope I find something I like," she says.

"I'm sure you will," I respond.

Hours later, we've cruised through about half of the mall, and my feet are killing me. I tell myself that next time, there is no way that I will wear my BCBG sandals when a lot of walking is involved. Then I look down at how cute they look and reconsider. Fashion is definitely worth the pain.

Nalini still has yet to buy anything, but she's got a pen and a piece of paper and is giving it all a lot of thought. She told me that she needs to make sure that what she buys is worth it, so she's decided to make a list of everything she wants, and then narrow it down to a few special items. The girl is more organized than I am! I could probably learn something from her. I make a mental note to start writing things down.

"Do you like the blue top or the purple one better?" asks Nalini, holding up two of the same tank tops in different colours.

"The purple one," I say. "It'll make your eyes sparkle."

"I think she should go with the blue," says a familiar voice from behind me.

I turn to look and should've known that the only person who would take any opportunity to disagree with me is Sonia.

"What're you doing here?" I ask through gritted teeth.

"Visiting my favourite cousin," responds Sonia, putting her arm around Nalini.

"Hi Sonia," Nalini grins. "You really like the blue one better?"

"Definitely, it's your colour," says Sonia, smirking at me.

"Well, I think any colour looks great on you," I say smiling at Nalini.

Nalini beams and then decides that she would rather put the purple top on the list.

As we walk out of the store, I notice Sonia following behind me. I make sure that Nalini is occupied with her list before continuing.

"What do you think you're doing?" I hiss.

"Shopping," she replies casually.

"Well, we're going this way," I point. "And you can go that way," I point in the opposite direction.

"I don't think so," she starts. "I've decided to join the two of you."

"What?" I exclaim. "You can't. We're having a day to ourselves. Why do you even want to?"

"Well, because," Sonia says with an evil grin. "It'll make you miserable."

An hour later, I've decided that Sonia is not going to get away with ruining my day. So far she's taken every opportunity to make me look foolish, from telling me that I have no idea what I'm talking about, to telling me I look fat in a pair of jeans. Even Nalini has noticed that something is wrong, which is the worst part. Today was supposed to make up for Nalini's birthday party being ruined. And instead, it's as if her birthday this year is just doomed.

I've come up with a plan called Operation Get Sonia Back and I'm just about to put phase one into action.

"What does everyone want to eat?" I ask as we find a table in the crowded food court.

"I want McDonald's," replies Nalini.

"I'll have a veggie sub," says Sonia snottily.

"Be right back," I say and head over to Mr. Sub.

"Hi, I'll have one small veggie sub with everything. Make sure you add extra jalapeno peppers, hot peppers, mushrooms, and olives," I say to the pre-pubescent boy behind the counter.

"Would you like to turn it into a meal?" he asks in his squeaky voice.

"She's definitely not worth it," I mutter under my breath.

"What?" he asks.

"Uh, no thanks," I reply.

I grab the sub, and two happy meals from McDonald's and make my way back to where they're seated with a smile on my face. Here goes phase one.

Sonia takes a bite of the sub, chews and her face immediately turns red. She grabs for my bottle of water and chugs half of it before she turns to me angrily.

"What the hell is wrong with you?" she asks through watery eyes. "I almost choked!"

"I don't know what you're talking about," I say innocently. No one, not even someone who can eat my mom's curry, could've handled that many peppers.

"You loaded this up with hot peppers!" she fumes.

"Well, I'm sorry, but that's how I eat my veggie subs," I shoot back at her. "I didn't know you wouldn't be able to handle it."

Nalini watches the exchange silently. Then she cries out between a mouthful of fries. "Sonia, what's happening to your face?"

Sonia reaches up to touch her face and shrieks in alarm. Her normally smooth face is slowly being covered in huge red welts.

"You're trying to kill me!" she yells at me, attracting the attention of a couple of people sitting near us.

"No I'm not," I say. "Keep your voice down and stop being such a baby, it was only a few peppers."

"Are there mushrooms on this?" she asks lowering her voice slightly.

"Yeah, but so what?" I say, not knowing what she's getting at.

"I'm allergic to mushrooms!" she says heatedly.

"No you're not," I say casually. "You're allergic to peanuts, shrimp, squash…" I trail off realising my mistake.

"And mushrooms!" she screams.

Sonia gets up from the table, grabs her purse and hurries out of the food court.

"Will she be okay?" asks Nalini, worried.

"She'll be fine. She just needs to get a shot," I say reassuringly.

It's me who's not going to be fine. Once this gets out, my whole family is going to think that I purposely tried to hurt her. I can just hear the way she'll tell it now.

"Jackie knows I'm deathly allergic to mushrooms and she tricked me into eating them because she's jealous of how much I've achieved." I look at Nalini and force a smile. Oh boy, I'm in trouble.

To Do List:

1. Find an apartment (one that doesn't smell)
2. Get a job (maybe something that will make me famous)
3. Take Nalini out (to make up for yesterday)
4. Clean my room (because it is starting to smell)
5. Pay phone bill (before they disconnect it)
6. Call Teresa (or else she'll kill me since we didn't talk at all yesterday)
7. Stop thinking about Shawn

The next morning, I cautiously creep down the stairs and brace myself. By now I'm sure that the whole Sonia situation has gotten around and I can already hear my parents yelling at me in their disapproving voices. I enter the kitchen to the smell of fresh *paranthas* and *achaar*.

"Good morning mom, dad," I say cheerfully.

"What happened yesterday?" asks mom grimly.

"I don't know, she had an allergic reaction," I say with a shrug.

"Who had a reaction?" asks mom in alarm.

Oh shoot, I assumed they already heard about it. Stupid me. What is the first rule of speaking to your parents when you know you've done something wrong? Never assume anything! Great, now I'm going to have to tell them.

"No one," I quickly lie.

"Don't give us that," says mom. "Who had an allergic reaction?"

"Okay, look," I start. "Sonia showed up at the mall and started to shop with us. When we went to go and eat, she ate some mushrooms and had a minor reaction to them."

"Why do you look guilty then," asks mom, knowingly.

Honestly, it's really unfair that she can read my mind like that, yet I can't read hers. Where is the justice in that?

"Fine," I say. "I brought her the sub with the mushrooms, so she's probably going around making it like I tried to kill her or something."

"*Beta*, you have to be more careful," dad says.

"I forgot!" I say defensively.

"Well, I'm sure she is fine now," says mom.

I look at her in shock. It's not like my mom to resolve a conflict without making sure that it hits its boiling point first.

"Uh, yeah," I say suspiciously. "I gave her a call last night to make sure." This is only half the truth. I did call her, but more to threaten her by telling her that if she told anyone some exaggerated story about what happened, then I'd make sure everyone found out that she was the one who put the dent in her dad's car last year.

"Good then, problem solved," says mom.

I can't take this anymore. I know she's letting me off the hook, but I have to know why she's going so easy on me.

"What's going on?" I ask.

"Nothing is going on," says mom casually. "Just make sure you don't forget about tomorrow. We are going to the *Mandir*."

"How can I forget?" I ask. "We've gone every Sunday since I can remember."

"Yes, well after the *Mandir* I expect you to be home," she states.

"Okay, why?" I ask curiously.

"I don't have to give you reasons. That is what I am telling you and that is it," she says sternly.

I start to argue with her, then decide against it. If she's in such a good mood, then I'm not going to be the one to ruin it.

"I'm going to lunch with Teresa today," I carelessly throw in.

"That is fine," says mom, and with that she gets up to do the dishes.

Later that day, Teresa and I are enjoying lunch at an expensive restaurant downtown.

I'm eating my favourite, Pasta Alfredo, while she's munching on something that looks like slimy snakes.

"What is that anyway?" I ask, totally grossed out.

"It's pieuvre, or in other words, octopus sautéed in some sort of sauce," she says matter-of-factly.

"Doesn't look too good," I respond.

"Well, I'm sorry you're not as cultured as I am," she teases.

I shrug and take another bite of pasta. "Hey, let's play our game!"

Teresa grins at me mischievously. "You start."

The two of us have come up with a game that we play whenever we go out to public places. It's actually very simple. We pick a guy and then grade him on a scale of one to ten and then state whether or not we'd sleep with him. It might sound childish and shallow, but it really does make for a fun afternoon. This one time, I'd given this guy a negative seven and said that the only way I'd sleep with him was if I was drunk and he wore a bag on his head. Unfortunately he overheard me. He must've had a great sense of humour though, because he told me to hurry and drink up while he ran out to grab a bag.

"That guy," I say, pointing to a short, stubby, balding man, standing by himself in the corner.

"Um, three and I wouldn't sleep with him," she says, wrinkling her nose.

"Three? I give him a one and only because that's the lowest grade. Look, he's picking his nose!" I cry out. I don't know why people stick their fingers in their noses in public. It's as if they think that there's an invisible force field around them and no one can see them.

"What about that one?" asks Teresa suddenly, nodding her head towards a tall, beefy, blonde man.

"Four and I'd probably only go to second base with him," I say grinning.

"Four?" asks Teresa. "He's hot! I'd give him an eight and I'd ask him how he likes it."

"Nah, not my style," I say shaking my head. "He's all yours."

"Nope, he's all that red-head's," says Teresa, frowning at the woman who just joined his table.

We order more drinks and I'm just finishing off my lunch when Teresa grabs my hand.

"I think I've found one for you," she says excitedly. "He's sitting by himself at the table diagonally across from us."

I look over, then immediately wish I hadn't. Sitting at the table, and looking even more handsome in broad daylight, is Shawn. And he's staring directly at me.

"Oh no!" I whisper. "It's Shawn!"

"That's Shawn?" asks Teresa in bewilderment. "Wow, when you said he's hot, I don't think you did him enough justice. This guy is the type you dream about."

"I've got to go," I say, ignoring Teresa.

"No, he's coming this way," she says.

I cast a look over my shoulder and realise that he's already standing at our table.

"Uh, hi, Shawn," I say trying to sound casual, yet failing.

"Jackie, how are you?" he asks.

I open my mouth to respond, but he interrupts me. "Listen, I'm sorry I never got a chance to call you back. I've been away on business all week and only just got back. I actually just wrapped up the final meeting with my clients."

"It's good, it's fine," I say with a wave of my hand.

"Hi, I'm Shawn," he says, noticing Teresa.

"I'm Teresa," she says fluttering her eyelashes and shaking his hand.

"Nice to meet you," he replies, before turning back to me. "I'd still like to buy you that drink sometime."

I stare at him a moment, caught off guard. I can't believe he still wants to take me out after the message I left him.

I find my voice and reply. "That sounds good."

"How about dinner tonight?" he asks hopefully.

"Okay," I respond.

"Great, I'll call you to get your address and pick you up around eight," he says with a quick smile. "Bye."

He nods to us both and turns to walk away. I look at the back of his frame and shiver. I've got a date with Shawn, tonight! It's amazing how fast things can happen. This morning I didn't expect to ever hear from him and now we've got plans. I'm so excited that I can't keep the goofy grin off my face. Then a thought hits me, what am I going to wear?

That night, as I'm applying my make-up, Teresa is standing by my bed, sorting through my clothes. She looks dishevelled and annoyed, but nevertheless happy for me. She offered to come and help me find the perfect outfit; unfortunately she's managed to confuse me more than ever.

"Teresa, it's okay. I think I can manage," I tell her.

"No, no. I can't leave until you're all ready," she insists.

I shrug and go back to applying some more lip-gloss. So far, we've narrowed it down to three outfits. A black Dolce & Gabbana skirt with a slinky purple tank top from Le Chateau, my Parasuco jeans with a low-cut white DKNY halter, or my funky, super short denim Guess skirt with a glittery pink tube top I got at a discount store. Personally, I think I'm going to have to nix the Guess skirt with the tube top. I want to look sophisticated and sexy, not trashy and easy. Teresa thinks that the outfit would show Shawn what could be his, and I keep insisting that there's no need to give away the goods so soon.

"Teresa, I can't do the Guess skirt," I say finally.

She pouts for a minute, and tosses the whole outfit into the reject pile. Then she turns to me.

"Fine, what would you like to wear?"

"I like the outfit with the black skirt," I start. "Don't you think it reeks sophistication?"

"Yeah, I was going to suggest that one next actually," she says with a nod.

I settle for that option and within a half hour, I'm dressed to perfection. Teresa gives me a once over and nods approvingly.

"You're going to knock his socks off," she says, giving me a quick peck on the cheek. "Now, I've got to be going. Gary is going to pick me up in an hour."

I raise my eyebrows. "The socks guy?"

Teresa and Gary have been very on again/off again for the last two months. We nicknamed him 'the socks guy' because he has an obsession with socks. They never match his outfit, he's got about a hundred pairs, and they're all very quirky. One time I caught him wearing socks up to his knees that were covered in strawberries.

"Yeah, I don't know, he's sort of cute in a really weird way," she says, thinking. "Anyway, he offered to take me to the movies, and since you're ditching me tonight, what choice did I really have?"

"Okay, enough with the guilt trip," I say, narrowing my eyes.

I walk Teresa to the door and wave goodbye to her. Then I see Shawn's car pull up into my driveway. I wait by the doorway for him and invite him inside. Luckily my parents are out for the evening, or else there's no way he'd be allowed inside, not unless I was marrying him or something.

"You're early," I say.

"Would you rather I came back in fifteen minutes?" he asks, jokingly. "By the way, you look very nice."

"Thanks," I blush. "So do you."

And I mean it. He's wearing a pair of dress pants and jacket with a crisp blue shirt underneath, sans tie. It makes him look very George Clooney, sexy and masculine.

"Let me just grab my purse," I say and hurry up the stairs.

When I come back down, he's glancing at the photos we keep above the fireplace mantle.

"Is this you?" he asks, pointing to a 5-year old version of me.

"Yes," I say with a smile.

"Cute," he smirks.

"Yeah, well I've changed just a bit since then," I say matter-of-factly.

"Really, you don't say," he jokes. "Shall we?"

I nod and follow him out to the car. The whole car ride is silent. I'm too nervous to speak and Shawn seems lost in thought. This isn't turning out quite the way that I'd hoped it would. First we start with small talk at my house, and then we don't speak in the car. I can only hope that I'm able to salvage the situation soon.

We arrive at a very fancy restaurant that I've never heard of before. There is an outdoor patio that is gleaming with lights. There are beautiful flowers, and a pond in the centre. The tables are covered with crisp white tablecloths and I can instantly tell that the silverware and china are expensive. One thing's for certain, this guy definitely knows how to treat a lady, and he must obviously have the cash to do so.

I try to take a seat at the table, but the waiter stops me and gives me a disapproving look. Then he pulls out the chair for me and seats me. Okay, so this place is a little bit more high class than the restaurants I normally go to. I decide to act as if I really do belong here.

"Can I get you something to start, Sir, Madam," asks the waiter. I notice it says Charles on his name badge.

"Yes, I'll have a glass of sweet sherry, Charles," I say in a fake English accent before I can stop myself.

Shawn gives me a quizzical look, and orders a glass of red wine. My cheeks burn red. I make a mental note to ditch the accent next time. And I can't believe I just ordered sherry. I don't even know what that is! I make another mental note to stop watching so many movies.

Shawn and I make small talk. I learn that he has two older siblings, one sister and one brother, both of whom are married with children. The drinks arrive and Shawn asks me if I'm ready to order. I nod. The truth is I haven't even had a chance to look at the menu yet. I've been sitting here, stressing and hoping that sherry isn't like pig's blood or something. I chance a quick sip and am relieved. Pig's blood or not, it doesn't taste bad.

"I'll have the Breton Bouillabaisse with a side of Spaetzle to start. And for the main course I'll have the Lapin à la moutarde," says Shawn in a perfect French accent.

I gulp. This guy seems way too cultured for me. And now Charles is looking expectantly at me.

"Same," I manage to squeak.

"Very good Madam," Charles nods, and turns to walk away.

While we wait for our dinner to arrive, I learn that Shawn has been working in public relations for about five years now. He's thirty and lives on his own. He moved from Vancouver to Toronto by himself when he was twenty-two. His parents still live in Vancouver and he visits them several times a year. I also learn that he's anxious to start his own business. Throughout all of this, I nod politely and ask questions at opportune moments. However, I'm finding the way the conversation is progressing slightly boring. I feel more like we've been set up by our parents, instead of having met at a club. Thankfully, our food arrives. I look down at the bowl being set in front of me and almost gag. It looks like some sort of a stew with chunks of grey meat floating around in it. I can also see some vegetables trying to poke through. A plate of thick bread slices is placed beside it. And in the centre of our table Charles places some sort of potato dumplings, which so far are the only things that look safe to eat.

"This looks good," I say in a fake voice of pleasure.

"Yeah, the food here is amazing," says Shawn. He picks up his spoon and starts to ladle portions of the stew on top of his bread. Then he grabs his fork and digs in.

I cautiously pour some of the soup onto the bread, trying to avoid the grey bits of meat. Shawn notices what I'm doing almost immediately.

"What's wrong? You don't like fish?" he asks.

Fish! I should've guessed that that's what it was. Personally, I have no problem eating fish. As long as it's covered in thick breading, like fish sticks. The thought of eating any of these slimy pieces of flesh grosses me out.

"Oh no, I've just never seen it look like this," I say.

"Probably because there's lots of assorted fish in that soup," says Shawn. "You know like mackerel, sardines, dover sole, eel."

Eel! I'm expected to eat eel? That's beyond disgusting. But instead of mentioning this, I say, "Fish tastes great. I um, just feel more like saving it until the end."

Shawn nods and continues eating. Fairly soon, our entrée's arrive and I push my uneaten fish bits aside, hoping against hope that the main course is edible.

It's worse than I expected. Sitting on a plate in front of me is some sort of creature, a rabbit I'm guessing by the size, or what used to be a rabbit. I stare at it, unsure of what I should do. I can't believe Shawn is actually going to eat this.

"Um," I start. "This is a rabbit, right?"

"Yep," replies Shawn, casting me a wary look. "Have you never had it before?"

"Well, not like this," I say slowly.

"Try it, you'll probably like it," says Shawn. "It tastes like chicken."

There is no way that I'm going to be able to eat what could have been some child's pet. I think of what I could do to get out of this, and decide that the only option that I have is to put it off as long as I can.

"I'll be right back," I say to Shawn.

"Are you okay?" he asks.

"Yeah, I just have to use the ladies room," I answer.

I get up from the table quickly, which causes me to accidentally knock my plate of the Easter Bunny onto the ground. I curse and look at the three waiters rushing to my side. One of them glares at me, before picking up my mess.

"I'm so sorry," I exclaim.

The other two are talking rapidly in French. I cast a sideways glance at Shawn, who has also stood up and is looking from me, to the food on the ground, to the waiters. Many of the other people in the restaurant have abandoned their meals to stare. A couple in the corner is giving me dirty looks and I overhear the woman say something about letting just anyone in here.

"Let me help," I offer.

I bend over to pick up the plate, and end up knocking over my glass of sherry. It hits the ground with a crash and shatters into pieces. I can feel my face turn red. I look at Shawn and my reflexes cause me to do the next worst thing. I grab my purse and run out of the restaurant.

When I reach the street corner, I stop. I hear Shawn's footsteps hurrying to catch up with me a minute later.

"Wow, well I guess that was a disaster," he says once he reaches me.

"You think?" I say.

Shawn stares at me a moment before opening his mouth to speak. "Look, I'm sorry. I tried to plan the perfect evening for us."

"Yeah, and I ruined it!" I exclaim.

"No, no, you didn't," he says. "I'm the stupid one who was nervous and tried too hard to impress you."

My ears perk up to this confession. "Why would you go out of your way to impress me?"

"Well, because there's something about you that I liked, right from when I first saw you," he admits reluctantly.

"Okay, now I know you're crazy," I say with a small laugh. "After the message I left you and the complete fool I just made out of myself, how can you still even want to be seen with me?"

Shawn laughs. "You should give yourself more credit. How about we redo this night?"

"I think that sounds like a great idea," I say.

"Just do me a favour," he requests.

I give him a questioning look.

"The next time I take you somewhere that's completely not your scene, tell me right away."

"Not my scene?" I ask trying to sound astonished. "I'll have you know that I come to restaurants like this all the time."

"Right, and do you always eat your bouillabaisse with your nose wrinkled in disgust," he teases.

"Yes, I do. It tastes better that way," I joke.

Shawn grabs my hand and we walk the rest of the way to his car in content, laughing about the disastrous evening. I guess the night didn't turn out to be a total mess after all.

The next morning, I wake up with a smile on my face. After the horrible incident at the restaurant, Shawn and I went to a little coffee shop that I know of and we ended up talking for hours. So far, he seems wonderful. He acted like a gentleman the whole night, which is more than I can say for a lot of guys I've dated. When he walked me up my driveway, he gave me an innocent kiss, instead of groping me in a drunken haze, as many of my past dates have done. And then he told me he'd call me soon, instead of telling me he'd see me around.

I shower and dress, feeling like I'm floating. I love first dates, when everything seems new, exciting and both people are extra nice to each other. Unfortunately, I know it won't last. I'm sure that within a couple of weeks, we'll have fought, or he might turn out to be a jerk. You can't blame me for thinking this way. After all, how many of the guys that I've dated in the past have turned out to be winners? Obviously none since I'm still single.

I wander down the stairs, pour myself a bowl of cereal and wait for my parents to finish getting ready so we can go to the *Mandir*. I don't have to wait long. I haven't even eaten all of my breakfast when they both come downstairs, bickering about something.

"I do not care if you don't want to," I hear mom telling dad. "I have already told Kulwinder and his wife that we will have dinner with them next weekend. And that is final."

"But Prabha, you know that I don't like those people," argues dad.

"You would make me go back on my word?" asks mom.

Dad thinks for a moment, trying to see if there's any way out of this. He looks at me for help and I shake my head no.

"Okay, fine," dad says reluctantly.

Mom turns to me with a look of triumph on her face and then stops to stare. "What are you wearing?"

"Um, my clothes for the *Mandir*," I answer slowly.

"Yes, but put on a nicer Indian suit," she says.

"I am wearing a nice one," I answer defensively.

"No, go and put on the peach one with the silver jewellery," mom orders.

"But why?" I ask, annoyed. "I don't have to dress up in order to pray."

"I know that," mom snaps.

I can tell she's going to blow pretty soon, so I decide to give up disputing and grudgingly go upstairs and change.

"And fix your hair and make-up," mom calls from downstairs.

At first I wonder why she's making such a big deal about how I look. Then I remember that this is my mother we're talking about. I can't ask questions because she has her quirky moments from time to time. I sum this up as one of those times and choose to take as long as possible, just to spite her.

Today we spend much longer at the *Mandir* than usual. Afterwards, both of them decide not to eat *prasad*, and I have no choice but to agree. By the time we arrive home, I'm starving and I immediately lunge for the fridge. But mom stops me and tells me not to touch anything just yet.

"Okay, what's going on?" I ask suspiciously.

"Nothing, I just think it will be better for us to eat together," says mom casually.

"But I'm so hungry," I whine.

I'm about to say more when I hear the doorbell ring. Mom claps her hands together in delight and disappears to answer the door. I can hear unfamiliar voices enter the house. I look at dad questioningly and he bows his head in guilt.

"Dad, who's at the door?" I ask, glaring at him.

"Um, *beta*, your, ah, mother set something up," he stutters.

"What?" I say, my voice rising.

"Well, your mother thinks, and I agree," he puts in as an afterthought, "that it wouldn't hurt for you to meet some boys."

"What?" I ask furiously. "And you're just throwing this all on me now? That's supposed to be one of my potential husbands out there waiting for me?"

Dad looks at the ground and I can immediately tell he had nothing to do with this. But before I can say more, mom rushes into the kitchen and orders me to make some *chai*. I look at her angrily and flat out refuse.

"You will make the *chai* and you will serve it," mom says sternly.

"No, I will not," I say heatedly. "So this is why you wanted me to look my best then?"

"Of course," answers mom. "I have been thinking about what you said the other day and you're right. You shouldn't be out of the house on your own. Therefore, it is time for you to find a husband, then you won't be alone," she says pointedly.

"Mom, there's no way I'm letting you set me up with someone, especially like this," I say through gritted teeth. "You deceived me. You didn't even have the decency to tell me."

"We will discuss this later. Right now, you will make the *chai* and be on your best behaviour. This is a very good family that you could go into. They are wealthy, Hindu, and he is a doctor," she says as if that settles the matter.

I look at her, almost hating her at the moment. Then I glance at dad to see if he can help me out. This time he shakes his head, avoiding my eyes. Mom then takes dad by his hand and leads him back to the living room to entertain the guests.

Fine! They want me to serve *chai* and be a good little Indian girl, just wait. I'll make sure that this is an occasion that they both regret.

While making the tea, I decide not to add enough tea leaves so that it tastes bland. Then I replace the sugar with salt to make sure that it is completely unbearable. I find this quite entertaining, since I actually can make a wonderful cup of tea. It's time for me to make my grand entrance. I consider sneaking back upstairs to put on a racy tube top and mini-skirt (no respectable Indian family would want their daughter-in-law dressed like that) but then think that maybe that's pushing it a bit too far. Instead I settle on being rude and indifferent when asked questions. I balance the tea on a tray with some snacks and cautiously make my way into the living room.

I set the tray down on the table and then take a seat on the sofa without saying a word. I sneak a quick look at Rich Boy and am actually sort of surprised. He's not bad looking. In fact, if our parents weren't setting us up, and had he approached me under different circumstances, I might even have flirted with him.

The parents of Rich Boy greet me and I flatly respond back. I notice mom pouring cups of tea for everyone, which is something that I was probably supposed to do. I wait anxiously, wondering who will be the first victim. Jackpot! My mom takes a sip and immediately spits it back into her cup. I know it's evil, but I can't help being a bit satisfied. I had really hoped that she would take the first sip. I mean it's not poison, it's just something to show her how angry I am. Mom shoots daggers at me with her eyes and then tells the family not to drink the *chai* because it needs sugar. They glance at her and then nod. Mom takes the cups from everyone and disappears into the kitchen to correct my error.

Then the family begins to ask me questions such as what my hobbies are, my age, you know the typical stuff that can be found on a resume for marriage. I give them quick one-word answers. From the corner of my eye, I see mom re-enter the living room with a fresh (and salt free I'm sure) pot of tea.

"So, what exactly do you do?" asks Rich Boy's mother, taking a cup.

"Well, at the moment, absolutely nothing," I say as if I'm so proud of myself.

Rich Boy's mother casts a quick look at her husband. I can tell that she's definitely not impressed.

"I'm sure that there is something that you would like to do then," she insists.

"Actually, nope," I respond. "I'm very happy just lazing around the house all day."

"So then you would enjoy being a housewife?" Rich Boy's father interrupts, as if he's figured me out.

"Nah, I can't cook, and I hate cleaning," I say wrinkling my nose.

Mom takes this opportunity to interrupt. "Kajal, she's joking," says mom with a laugh. "She is a wonderful cook and you should see her room, spotless."

Rich Boy's father nods in approval. "Of course I knew she must be making a joke."

The parents finally introduce us. I learn that his name is Ravi, and they think that this would be an appropriate moment for me to take him on a tour of our house. I think that this could actually turn out well. What better way for me to make sure they run from the house screaming? I'll just act like a total jerk towards their son.

"So, Ravi is it?" I ask while walking up the stairs.

"That's right," he answers casually.

"What exactly is it that you do?" I ask snottily.

"I'm a doctor," he says with a hint of pride.

"Oh, so you think that that's something super special, do you?" I throw back.

He smirks. "This is coming from someone who has no job at all?"

I stare at him a second, at a loss for words. So he wants to play, does he?

"I do have a job," I lie. "I just didn't want to tell your parents."

"Oh?" he asks, raising his eyebrows.

"Yeah, I work for the government," I answer as we walk down the hallway. "I'm actually on a very top secret assignment right now."

Ravi laughs at this. "You really expect me to believe that? You've got to be kidding."

"Actually, I don't really care if you believe me or not," I say coldly.

"Well, that's a relief then," he says sarcastically.

I can't believe this guy! What a jerk. It's time to put an end to this tour. But before I can shoot back a rude answer, he interrupts me.

"Look, to be quite honest, I have no desire to be here right now," he says, crossing his arms and leaning against the wall. "You seem like you could be a nice girl if you dropped the whole act and grew up a bit. But it wouldn't matter, because I've got a serious girlfriend."

"You do?" I ask, incredulously.

"Yep," he nods.

"Well then why are you here?" I wonder.

"Why are you here?" he responds. "Obviously we've both been put in this awkward situation because of our parents."

"So why don't you tell them that you have a girlfriend and save yourself from being put through these awkward situations," I shoot back, my hands on my hips

"Why are you so interested?" he asks slyly.

Of all the conceited, annoying guys that I've met, this one definitely tops the list. "I'm not!" I answer huffily.

"Good, then let's head back downstairs," he suggests.

"Yes, lets," I agree. "Also, a word of advice, do tell your parents that there is no need for them to continue finding you a wife, if for no other reason than to save another poor girl the trouble of having to meet you."

This time I've left Ravi at a loss for words. Then he shrugs and heads back down the stairs. I follow him, but keep a safe distance behind. He whispers something to his dad and his dad tells mine that he doesn't think that this relationship will work out. Within no time, the family has left our house. I lean back against the wall, relieved for the time being. Then I realise that I better get out of my mom's sight, because if I know her, she's not going to let this go easily.

To Do List:
1. Yell at parents for putting me through such a horrific event
2. Pay my phone bill...seriously this time
3. Clean my room before the smell moves in permanently
4. Stop checking phone every ten minutes to see if Shawn has called

Much later that night, after Ravi and his family have left and I'm alone with my family, we're all eating dinner. My dad keeps glancing from me to my mom, probably wondering which side he should take. My mom has decided to give me the silent treatment, and for now I'm going to let her, at least until I've finished eating. There's no sense in getting upset on an empty stomach.

Once the dishes are cleared, my parents leave me to wash them and wander away to watch yet another

Indian movie. As I'm soaping the plates, my anger and frustration continue to build. I just don't understand how two people can be as different as my mom and I. She has the most surreal way of thinking. I mean, first I'm being ordered to move out because she insists that I need to be more independent. Then she completely changes her mind and decides that I should get married. Isn't that totally contradicting herself? When did I ever tell her that I wanted to get married anyway? If anything, I've told her quite the opposite. Perhaps this is her way of easing the pain of me living on my own, by pressuring me to marry a stranger. Yeah, that sounds like a fabulous idea to me.

When I've finished rinsing, I've come to a conclusion. There really is only one thing for me to do from here, I tell myself as I enter the living room. I can see the hero and heroine in the movie performing a song and dance number on the screen. It's funny how all of the villagers have coordinated outfits, and know all the dance moves. I take a deep breath and prepare myself for what I'm about to say.

"Mom, dad," I start. "I'm moving out."

They both look at me quizzically. Mom raises her eyebrow at dad and he shrugs. "We know you are," she says. "We're the ones who asked you to."

Okay, not quite the reaction I was looking for. "No, what I mean is that I'm moving out now." I say seriously.

They both continue to give me blank stares and I realise that it's time for a longer explanation.

"Look, you both asked me to move out so that I could be more independent, right?" I ask. "Well, I also know that neither of you actually really expected it to happen. I mean, sure, you told me to move out, find a job, whatever. But you thought it would take weeks, maybe even months. And the only reason that you said it in the first place is to try to scare me into doing something real with my life." I stop to take a breath and wait for a reaction.

Dad looks at his hands and mom nods slowly.

"So," I continue. "It's time. I'm serious. I can't continue to live in this house with the thought that another potential suitor might make a surprise visit. I've had it. I'm going to make something of myself because neither of you take me seriously nor really think that I can." I finish dramatically.

Mom stares intently and dad still looks at the ground.

"So, you think that you will do better living by yourself instead of getting married?" challenges mom.

"Yes, I do," I answer confidently. "Besides, where did this come from anyway? I thought that you wanted me to be independent."

"We do," dad finally puts in. "But *beta*, think of how hard it will be. At first we thought it would be better for you to live on your own. But then we thought it would be too much. You need to have someone to support you."

At hearing this, I glare at them both menacingly. "So, neither of you believes in your daughter. You both think that I'm some pathetic little girl who needs to rely on someone."

"No *beta*," starts my dad upon realising what he's said.

"Forget it dad," I interrupt. "I understand clearly now. Neither of you wants to have me as a burden in your life. So first you figured it'd be easier to ask me to move out. Then you felt guilty and you decided to just marry me off so that at least I wouldn't turn into a beggar on the streets or something. Well don't worry because I'll be gone within twenty-four hours and trust me, I will succeed."

I don't wait for either of them to respond. The hurt and anger take over and I give them both one last look before storming off to my room and slamming the door.

Screwed, I am totally screwed. I now realise that I might've overreacted just a tad bit. I probably shouldn't have gone on a rampage and told my parents that I'd be gone within a day, especially since I have nowhere to go. I consider going back downstairs to apologize, but then my pride steps in the way. Okay, it's time to think seriously. I've already called Teresa and told her the whole story. She generously offered to let me stay at her house until I find a place of my own, which I had to accept. Great, I'm trying to be more independent and the first thing that I do is crash at a friend's house. Really good start Jackie, I congratulate myself. I look around my room and grab a suitcase. I have no choice but to start packing.

I hear a knock on my door that brings me out of my thoughts. I answer it to find my dad standing on the other side.

"I wanted to come and give you this," he says, shoving an envelope in my hand.

I open it to find a wad of cash peeking out at me.

"I can't take this," I say, giving it back to him.

"Since when can you not take something that your father is giving you?" he asks me.

"Does mom know?" I shoot back at him.

Dad looks at the ground sheepishly, which tells me that she has no clue.

"I'll be fine dad," I say. "I have a little bit of money in my savings, and besides this is a chance for me to make something of myself."

"*Beta*, I know that. But still, I have never ordered you to do anything. Right now I am ordering you to take this money and that is final," he says sternly.

Hearing dad speak to me so firmly surprises me at first. Then I can see worry in his eyes and I soften up. I take the envelope, promising myself not to use it unless I desperately need it, and then hug him. "I'll be fine," I whisper.

The following morning, I've got my things packed and am waiting at the front door. My mother and father are standing by my side. They both tried to make me change my mind. They even went so far as to forbid me to leave, but I'm firm in what I believe. I need to be more independent and assertive so that I can go after what I really want. Perhaps this is the only way for me to find my true calling.

Dad looks as if he's on the verge of tears, and even mom looks upset at having to see me go. She's holding a *pooja* tray in her hand, because she's trying to ward off any evil that might come my way. She leans forward and puts a *bindi* on my forehead, then nods, telling me that it's safe for me to go. I hug them quickly, knowing that if I stay much longer I might change my mind. I look at my parents, knowing that from this day forth things will be very different, and then I turn to leave the house.

Part 2:
When The Going Gets Tough...

What Job is perfect for you?
1.   What are your hobbies?
     I like to watch t.v, shop, attend social events

2.   Where do you see yourself in ten years?
     I see myself being a huge success and traveling the world

3.   What subjects interested you most in school?
     Art, Drama, Gym

4.   On a scale of one to ten rate the following in importance:

     The amount of money you make: *10*
     Working long hours: *5*
     Your ambition: *6*
     Teamwork: *2*
     Your goals and accomplishments: *6*

Results:
     Based on your responses, you would do well to work independently in a small shop, or perhaps

start your own business. You should stick to working within industries such as fashion, interior design, or travel.

Teresa suggested that I take an online quiz to see what sort of career I should pursue, even though I told her that I'm through with taking these tests because they always make me feel like a moron. This one wasn't so bad, although it wasn't very informative. How can I start my own business without any money? I'd be in debt for a long time before I started to make a profit, which is not the way I see myself succeeding. Besides, who in their right mind would give a loan to someone who has no job or assets and a bunch of bills and student loans to pay? Maybe the quiz thought that I was a rich heiress or something. Now that sort of lifestyle I could definitely get used to. I'd have people treating me with respect and waiting on me all day long while I sipped martinis by a pool. I could shop as much as I wanted and never have to worry about working or paying bills. I wouldn't have to live on my own because I'd have hired help surrounding me. I could even get one of those cute little dogs as my permanent companion and she would fit inside my Luis Vuitton bag. I'd name her Princess and she'd be the most well kept and cared for puppy ever. I think Teresa's had the right mind set all along. I should just marry rich. Then I could do as I chose all day long, while my husband took care of everything.

Perhaps I should seriously consider this...or at least get a dog or something.

Much later that night, Teresa and I are sitting in her basement, which has become my temporary living quarters, and drinking margaritas. We both decided that I've had enough stress for one day and that I should take the night off to enjoy myself, because it's all work starting tomorrow.

"So, what're you planning on doing now?" asks Teresa.

"Well, today I already called like twenty companies and basically I had to beg them to give me an interview," I say a little ashamed. "I told them I'd be willing to do anything, even filing or getting coffee. Luckily I found one that said they did have an opening so I'm going to talk to them about it tomorrow."

"Good job!" Teresa smiles encouragingly. "I'm sure once they meet you, they'll hire you on the spot."

"Yeah, now I just need to find a place to live," I say.

"Well, no rush," she says with a wave of her hand. "You can stay here as long as you like. Mom and dad insisted. You know that they consider you an honorary daughter."

"That's so sweet," I reply sincerely. I adore Teresa's parents. They're like the Ken and Barbie of the real world. Her mom, Jill, works as a teacher in a middle school and is absolutely stunning to look at. Teresa's dad, Mitch, is a lawyer (not the fake kind that Sonia brags about being, but a real one who deals with criminals) who makes more money than I've known my entire life. They make the perfect couple.

"So, what's up with Shawn?" asks Teresa.

"I don't know," I frown. "He hasn't called."

"Well, it's only been two days. I'm sure you'll hear from him soon enough," she says. "Besides, he told you how busy he is with work and stuff."

"Yeah," I agree. "Ugh, I can't believe that my parents tried to set me up with that jerk, Ravi."

"I know, what a weirdo," she responds, wrinkling her nose.

"I feel bad for his girlfriend," I joke. "Hey, speaking of weirdo's, what's going on with you and Gary?"

"Hey," she says defensively. "He's not that weird."

"I just like bugging you about him," I laugh.

Teresa rolls her eyes. "Well, I don't know what's going on. Nothing, I guess."

"Yeah but you guys have been randomly dating for a couple months now," I continue.

"That doesn't mean anything," Teresa insists. "He's nice enough, but I don't know. We'll see I guess."

"What's the problem?" I ask. "Aside from the fact that he loves his socks."

Teresa shakes her head at me, but is grinning. "You're so bad. Well, there is no problem. I'm just trying to figure out whether I really like him or not, I guess, and also whether he really likes me."

"Well, what's not to like?" I ask. "You're hot, smart, super nice, and he's a nice guy and rich."

"Yeah, you forgot one thing," starts Teresa. "He's not that great looking."

"And this is the only thing that's stopping you?" I inquire.

"Well, I mean I have to be attracted to him, don't I?" responds Teresa. "So what if he's tall and has good hair? He has those thick rimmed glasses that he insists on wearing with that string around his neck, he has the sock obsession, and he's built a little too wiry for my liking."

"And you say that I'm picky," I laugh.

Teresa shrugs and then turns on the TV. I can tell that this conversation is over for the moment. I hear Teresa shriek in delight and realise that one of our favourite movies, A Night at the Roxbury, is playing. I sink back into the couch to watch and sip my margarita, all other thoughts temporarily pushed from my mind.

The next morning, I'm sitting patiently in an office, waiting my turn to be interviewed. I'm actually nervous and can't stop fidgeting, which I'm sure isn't a good thing. I can see the receptionist staring at me from over her paperwork. I try to smile at her, after all this could be my future co-worker, but she glares at me and goes back to her paperwork. What the heck is her problem? I ignore her for now and suddenly wish that I'd asked more questions about what sort of job I'm applying for. For all I know they could ask me to dissect animals for lab testing or something. That'd be horrible! What sort of sick people use animals for testing? If they expect me to do that, there's no way. And I think that I'll tell them off before I leave as well. But, this doesn't really look like the sort of place that could have animals in the back, I try to reassure myself. Then again, what do I know?

I feel so unprepared, and there is a woman sitting across from me, looking very professional, and totally put together. She's sitting up tall, her hands folded neatly in her lap, her make-up perfect, and not a hair out of place. I'm sure that she is also here for the interview and this only helps to make me more fidgety. I should've spent longer getting ready. I bet my eyeliner is smudged and why didn't I bring my hairbrush? I take a calming breath and give myself a pep talk. I know I can do this job, whatever it is. I've never failed at anything yet, at least not anything that I was hell bent on doing, which now that I think of, hasn't been much. In fact, I can't seem to recall the last time that I really wanted to do something, other than going out on a Saturday night. My last job was months ago and I was always late, or calling in sick. What is wrong with me? Why am I such a screw up? I'm twenty-four years old and I have nothing to show for it. It's as if my life thus far hasn't made any difference at all. I can feel myself starting to panic. The woman sitting across from me must have noticed because she leans across and pats my hand gently.

"First time?" she asks.

"No, actually it's just been awhile," I reply back.

"It's okay, it takes some getting used to," she responds, smiling. "Don't be nervous."

"I can't help but be a little," I say with a small laugh.

"Well, they're all really nice here," she reassures.

"You've been here before?" I ask, surprised. How many times has this woman come in for an interview?

"Yeah, it's my third time," she answers. "But they're so great here that I could keep coming back forever."

"Really," I respond. Wow, she must want this job more than I do!

"Well, you know," she starts. "Once you find a great therapist, it's always best to stick to them."

Therapist? What is she talking about? Then it dawns on me. I'm in a psychiatrist's office! I can't believe I didn't notice before. This woman isn't my competition. She's here to see a therapist. This immediately calms my nerves. She's not a threat to me after all.

"So what're you here for anyway, if you don't mind me asking," she inquires.

Luckily at that moment a short man with a bulging belly tells me that they're ready to see me. I breathe a sigh of relief, grateful that I don't have to tell the woman that I'm not here for the same reason she is. I feel that this might embarrass her.

"Nice meeting you," I say to her before rushing to follow the man.

I enter a side office and take a seat. The short man sits across from me and introduces himself as Tom Burns, head of the facility.

"Now Jackie, we're currently hiring for an office assistant, which means that you'd be responsible for filing, typing up documents, and taking over receptionist duties when needed, among other things," says Tom.

"Okay," I nod.

"Do you have any experience?" asks Tom.

"Absolutely," I reply enthusiastically. I leave out the fact that the only office experience that I had was a two-month job as a secretary where I was constantly late, always on the phone and then fired for sending out a memo to all of the bosses with a typo in it. I know that sounds harsh, but actually it wasn't since the sentence I typed out was, "I have f***ed over Mr. Norton's process reports," instead of "faxed over." I think I was talking to Teresa while I was typing the memo. Silly me.

"What sort of job was it?" Tom asks, raising his eyebrows slightly.

"Well, I worked in a manufacturing company as a secretary, so I had many of the same responsibilities that you've just described," I say confidently.

"That sounds good," Tom encourages. "Now, this is a fulltime position and we pay you on an hourly rate for the first three months. Afterwards, you will have a review and if we decide to keep you on, then you'll be switched over to salary and may apply to receive benefits."

"I understand," I nod again. I realise that I haven't really said much and think that maybe I should ask some questions so that he knows I'm not stupid.

"And how long is lunch?" I ask before I can stop myself. Shoot, wrong question. Now he's going to think that all I care about is how much free time I'll have.

"You get an hour," Tom says with a laugh.

Thank God, he's got a sense of humour. I breathe a small sigh of relief but decide not to chance it again and go back to saying as little as possible.

"Do you have any other questions?" he asks.

Is it just my imagination, or is he mocking me? I can see a twinkle in his eye as if he's trying not to laugh again.

"Um, no," I reply.

"Well, I guess there really isn't much else to explain, since the position is pretty self explanatory. We'll call you within a few days to let you know," says Tom, standing up to shake my hand.

Wait, it's already over? I don't think I made quite the right impression. I wish he would've asked me why I wanted this job. Then I could go on about how dedicated I am to making something of myself and how I really felt I could succeed in the position. But before I can say anything else, I've already been ushered out into the hall. I stand for a second and then figure there's nothing else I can do, so I make my way through the waiting room and out the front doors. Great, there goes that one.

Jackie,
I'll be out for a couple of hours with Gary. Feel free to eat, lounge, do whatever. Make yourself at home! Mom and dad won't be back from work

until around six but I should be home before then.
Hope the interview went well, and I can't wait to
hear all about it! See you soon babe.
Love ya,
Teresa
PS. Call your mom! She called for you at 9:30am,
10:25am and 11:45am.

I get to Teresa's to find myself completely alone, which doesn't help my mood. I can only hope now that I get the job. I realise that I need to de-stress and decide to take a hot bubble bath and then call my mom, since apparently she's been stalking me. Not only did she call Teresa's, but she left two messages on my cell phone as well. Oh no, I hope I don't turn into one of those people who only gets calls from their mother. Maybe I'll become one of those sad old women who live on their own with nothing but cats for company and who yell at the neighbour's kids for no reason at all. Then my mom will come and visit, and bring food with her since I'm too hopeless to make anything myself. I catch a glimpse of myself in the mirror and see that I'm frowning. Even worse, now I'm going to have premature wrinkles from all this worrying. I turn my frown into a smile and then sink into the bath.

I don't know how much later, it could've been ten minutes or three hours, but I hear my phone ringing. Mom again, I think. But I figure that I might as well get ready now and call her before she begins to worry.

I mean I don't want to end up being the cause of her wrinkles as well.

When I'm all dressed, I pick up my phone to a pleasant surprise. It was actually Shawn who called me. I listen to his message and feel a shiver go up my spine. This guy sounds hotter every time I hear from him. He tells me to call him back when I get a chance. Damn, why did I have to miss his call? I wonder if it seems too desperate for me to call him right now. I glance at the time and nix the idea because it has only been ten minutes since he called. Maybe I should play it his way and wait a couple of days. Then again, I don't want him to think that I'm playing games. Although, I could be really busy, he doesn't know. For all he knows, it could always take me a few days to call someone back. Then again, he does know that I'm unemployed, and that I have a lot of free time on my hands. I shake my head in frustration. Where is Teresa when I need her? I throw the phone on the bed and decide to leave it there until I speak to her. If I take it downstairs with me, I might be tempted to call. The worst would be if I had to leave him a message. I shudder as I think of the way that went last time. No, definitely need to speak to her before I call him.

Then it hits me. What am I doing? I'm acting like one of those immature girls who over analyze everything. I mean, is it me whose going to have the relationship with Shawn, or Teresa? I laugh at the thought, and then stop myself because I feel like I'm starting to act a little crazy. Well, that's not so bad since I might be working at a therapist's office. Perhaps they give free sessions to their employees. Wait, I'm getting totally off topic. Right, so I need to pick up my phone and call Shawn back. No playing games, no thinking twice. I'll do what I feel like doing when I feel like doing it, and make my own decisions. Now that that's settled, I dial his number before I can change my mind.

"Hello," I hear his sexy voice answer on the second ring.

"Hi, Shawn," I say casually. "It's Jackie, sorry I just missed your call."

"Hey, Jackie," he says smoothly. "I should be the one who's sorry. I swear I wanted to call you like the next day but had to fly unexpectedly to New York for some business."

"Not a problem," I respond lightly.

"So how've you been?" he asks.

Fantastic, I think silently. I got into a fight with my parents because they tried to force me into marriage and then I moved out of my house in a fury. Now I'm mooching off my friend and I think I just bombed my first job interview. "Oh I've been good," I say instead.

"Would you like to go out for dinner tonight? I promise no more snooty restaurants," he jokes.

"Well, only if you promise," I reply with a laugh.

"Great, I'll pick you up around seven," Shawn confirms.

"Perfect, see you then," I say, getting ready to hang up. Then I remember something. "Wait! Um, you'll have to pick me up from my friend's house." I say in a rush. I give him the address. Then we both hang up.

I'm glad he didn't ask too many questions about why he would be picking me up from Teresa's. Hopefully he just assumes that I had plans to be at her house from before. I wonder if I should tell him the truth when I see him. It definitely might be a downer during dinnertime. Maybe for now, I'll just tell him a more interesting story. Like, I had to come to her house to make posters because we're volunteering for a rally to help save the rain forest. That would definitely be more fun and plus it'd make me look like a good person. No, Jackie, I tell myself. Honest. I have to be honest with him if I want this to go anywhere.

All of a sudden, my phone rings again. This time it's my mom. I really should've called her first. I'm sure she'll complain about that fact.

"Hello," I answer.

"Janaki, you didn't call back yet. I have been sick with the worry," my mom nags me.

"Is everything okay?" I ask.

"Of course it is. You think to only call if something is wrong? You should be calling always," mom insists.

"I'm sorry. I'll make sure I call more often in the future," I roll my eyes.

"Do not be sarcastic," mom snaps. "I know that tone of voice."

How does she always know? "Mom, did you just call to yell at me?"

"No, I wanted to make sure you're okay," she says, softening her voice slightly. "You know I'm not your enemy."

"I know mom. Like I said, I'm sorry I didn't call you back yet. And everything is going well. I had an interview this morning, so I'm keeping my fingers crossed," I tell her, trying to change the subject.

"Good for you," mom encourages.

Sometimes I can't handle my mom's mood swings. One minute she's badgering and snapping at me, and the next minute she's cheering me on.

"Thanks mom. I'll call you again later okay?" I say reassuringly.

"Okay, then. Bye. Be safe," says mom with a click of the phone.

Within a couple of hours, I get a sense of déjà vu as Teresa is standing in front of me with her hands on her hips, and her eyebrows scrunched together in thought. She's once again trying to help me pick out an outfit and as usual, we've come up with a few different ones. What is unusual though is that we've both been in agreement thus far.

"Now that I think about it, the black capris won't look that good with the sequined red top," says Teresa matter-of-factly. She puts her finger to her mouth, thinking, and then her eyes brighten. "I've got it! The red top with the dark blue Guess jeans. You'll totally knock him down when he sees you dressed so hot."

"Thanks babe. I knew you were my friend for a reason," I smile, running the flat iron through my hair. "I wonder where he's going to take me tonight."

"Ohhh, maybe that new Italian restaurant. You know how hard it is to get in there? Luke has been trying to make reservations for the two of us for weeks," says Teresa, and then she claps her hand over her mouth.

"Luke?" I ask in surprise. "As in your ex-boyfriend Luke?"

If there was an award for the two most incompatible people, Teresa and Luke would win by a long shot. He's the most arrogant, mouthy, jerk I've ever come across, and I totally hate him for what he did to her. They dated for over a year and were talking about moving in together. Then he left her for some other blonde girl the day they were supposed to go condo hunting. I had no idea that he was back in the picture.

"Why are you talking to him?" I ask accusingly.

"I didn't want to tell you, because I didn't think anything would happen," Teresa says guiltily. "He called me like two weeks ago, told me that he'd been stupid and that there wasn't a day that went by that he didn't regret what he did."

"Teresa, have you completely lost your senses? Do you not remember what he put you through when he left you?" I ask. All thoughts of getting dressed leave my mind.

"I know, I know," starts Teresa looking at the floor. "But he told me he missed me, Jackie."

"If he told you he was going to buy you a car would you believe him as well?" I shoot back. I know I might be being a little harsh, but these are things that she needs to hear. I can't stand the thought of her getting hurt by him again. The first time it devastated her for months. She locked herself in her room for days on end. If she had to go through that again, I don't know what she'd do this time.

"I knew you would think of it this way," Teresa says. "But I really think that it'll be different this time."

"Yeah, maybe this time he'll go off with a red head instead," I say sarcastically.

Teresa looks at me, tears welling up in her eyes. "Look, I know you're only saying that because you care about me, but do you have to be so mean about it? Can't you just attempt to be happy for me?"

I soften at her words and then sit beside her on the bed. "I'm sorry," I say putting my arm around her. "It's just that I don't want you to get hurt again Teresa, because when you get hurt, it also hurts me."

"Jackie trust me," she says with a small smile. "I know what I'm doing."

"Okay," I say with a nod. "Is this why you're so unsure about Gary?" I ask suddenly.

"Well, not only this, but I guess that it does have something to do with it," Teresa says with a shrug.

I hear my cell phone ring, which interrupts our conversation. I reach over to grab it and recognize Shawn's number.

"Hello," I answer.

"Hey, I'll be there in five minutes," Shawn tells me.

Five minutes! I need at least another twenty to get ready. "Uh, sure, see you then," I tell him and hang up.

"Is that Shawn?" asks Teresa.

I can tell by the tone of her voice that what we were just discussing has come to an end. I make a note to bring it up again later.

"Yeah, he's going to be here in a few minutes and I'm not even ready," I say quickly.

"No prob," Teresa says with a wave of her hand. "I'll keep him company downstairs while you finish getting dressed."

"Thanks a lot," I say, hugging her. I hold on to her for an extra second. "And just remember that I'm always behind you."

Shawn and I are seated at a nice, yet not overly posh restaurant later that night. We just ordered our dinner; mine is actually food that I recognize and have eaten before. I take a sip of my wine and then lean a bit closer, showing him that I'm paying one hundred percent attention to what he's saying. The truth is that I have no idea what he's talking about because he's talking about his work. I got as far as he had a huge merger to take care of in New York and then he lost me, but I continue to nod here and there so he doesn't think I'm completely stupid.

"So, you see, it's all really simple when you look at it," he finishes triumphantly.

"Yeah, I believe you," I reply, not knowing what else to say.

"And you have no idea what I was just talking about," he puts in, his mouth twitching in amusement.

"None what-so-ever," I agree, shaking my head.

"Well, it was worth a try," he shrugs. "Next time, I'll be sure to keep my work talk short and sweet."

"Oh thank God," I tell him gratefully. "I mean, no offence or anything."

"None taken," he says. "So why don't you tell me what you've been up to?"

I look from him, to the floor and then back to him again. I knew that this would be coming. And I do plan on telling him the truth. I just haven't figured out yet how much of the truth I can tell him without scaring him or something.

"Well, I went to the *Mandir* with my parents like we always do," I start. And before I know it, I've spilled out the whole story, from Ravi, to being stressed about having to find an apartment, to my interview this morning. It actually feels really good to be able to tell Shawn everything. I finish and then wait for him to comment.

"Wow, you've had a rough couple of days so I see," he says. Then he starts to laugh. "I can't believe your parents wanted you to marry a complete stranger! I mean I know that it's Indian custom, but I guess that I've just been raised in a very Westernized family. It still amazes me to think that stuff like this still happens on this side of the world."

"I know," I nod in agreement.

Our dinner arrives and I can smell the authentic Italian spices in my pasta. My mouth waters in delight and I pick up my fork to dig in. For a few minutes we eat comfortably in silence.

"You know," Shawn starts suddenly. "One of my client's is actually looking to sublet his place."

"Really?" I ask. I can't believe that he's offering to help me find a place to live.

"Yeah, I've been looking for a new place of my own and I think I'm going to take it," he adds.

"Oh," I say in surprise.

"I'm kidding," Shawn says with a laugh. "I meant for you. If you want, I can set it up so that you can check it out, and see if you like it. Since you know me, he'll probably make the rent really cheap."

"Oh that'd be great," I say breathing a sigh of relief. "And FYI, I knew you were joking."

"Sure you did," Shawn winks.

I sit back, my smile growing bigger as the evening wears on. I think this guy could actually be a keeper.

To Do List:
1. Keep looking for a job, anything at this point will do
2. Call mom before she calls me
3. Get a hold of Shawn to make sure he's taking me to see the apartment
4. Clean Teresa's house so she knows how thankful I am…actually on second thought, maybe I'll write her a note or something

It's late afternoon and I'm sitting in Teresa's living room, waiting for Shawn to pick me up. He talked to his friend, Mark, and we're going to head over to the apartment to check it out. I just hope that everything goes well and the place doesn't have cockroaches or something. As long as there's nothing terribly wrong with it, I'm going to take it on the spot. Although I love Teresa and truly appreciate what her family is doing for me, two days of living at her house is driving me crazy! Last night I was watching TV in the living room and I could hear her parents arguing loudly in the kitchen. Apparently Mitch was staring at some cashier in the grocery store and Jill was not too happy about it. Then much later at night, I came upstairs from the basement to make myself a cup of tea, and I could hear them from all the way upstairs in their bedroom, making up. I don't think I've ever been so embarrassed in my life, in fact, I completely forgot about my tea and ran as fast as my legs would carry me back downstairs.

I hear my cell phone ring and immediately answer it, assuming that it's Shawn telling me that he's running late or something. I'm totally unprepared for who's on the other end.

"Hello, may I speak with Jackie Malhotra," asks an unfamiliar voice.

"Speaking," I answer, trying to sound professional.

"Hi, this is Tom Burns. You had an interview with us yesterday," he says.

"Oh yes. Hello. How are you?" I say trying to sound as pleasant as possible.

"I'm good and yourself?" he asks.

"Absolutely spiffing," I respond, remembering a line I once heard in a movie. I wait a beat to see what he's going to say next.

"Well, I guess I'll get straight to the point Jackie. I'm calling to offer you the job that you were interviewed for," says Tom.

"Oh my God, are you serious?" I exclaim. All thoughts of trying to sound professional are out of my head. "Thank you so much!"

"So I guess this means that you'll take it," Tom says with a laugh.

"Hell yes, err, I mean of course," I say before I can stop myself.

"Well I'm glad to hear it," Tom continues. "So we'll see you in the office on Monday morning, 8:30am sharp."

"Sounds good," I respond, trying to calm myself down. "You have yourself a great day Mr. Burns."

"You too Jackie, and please call me Tom," he says before hanging up.

I switch my phone off and sit for a second in shock. Then I stand up and do a sort of jig before jumping up and down in delight. My problems are solved. I have a job. I must have made quite an impression yesterday. It crosses my mind that I'm not really qualified for the job but I push the thought out of my head. I'm sure I can learn quickly. I need to make sure I thank Tom properly when I see him on Monday. I know he won't regret hiring me.

"Do you always dance when you're happy?" I hear Shawn ask me from behind.

"Um, yes, I, ah, feel that it helps to keep one young," I answer, my face turning red in embarrassment.

"So what made you so happy today?" he asks with a twinkle in his eye.

I consider saying something flirty in a sexy, breathless voice like, "The fact that you're here," but then nix this idea because I know I could never pull it off. Plus I think that after the little dance number I just put on, I've humiliated myself enough for one day. "I just got the job!" I exclaim instead.

"Congratulations," Shawn says enthusiastically, giving me a quick kiss.

"So what, you're just walking into houses?" I ask coyly.

"Actually I was let in. I think your friend's dad," Shawn explains.

"Oh, I see," I respond. "So shall we head over to the apartment?"

"Sure," says Shawn. He leads me outside and into his car. "Listen, I need to warn you about something though," he starts while putting the car into reverse.

"Okay. Wait don't tell me. The place is covered in roaches," I say, imagining my worst fear coming true.

"Nah, only in the winter," Shawn jokes.

"So what then? Mark changed his mind and doesn't want to rent anymore? The faucets leak? The apartment is painted in all black? No, no, I've got it. There's mouldy furniture. I knew it. I'm going to have to spend all of my money redecorating," I finish dramatically.

"Are you done?" Shawn asks, raising his eyebrow slightly.

"I think so," I say taking a deep breath.

"Okay, so it's like this," Shawn starts. "I had to tell Mark that you're my fiancée. It's the only way that I could make sure that he'd give you a good deal."

"What?" I ask in shock. "I don't know if I'm comfortable with this. Couldn't you just tell him that we're really good friends or something?"

"Well, I could've," Shawn says slowly. "But this way, it also ensures that he won't hit on you either."

I can't help but smile. "Jealous?" I ask with a smirk.

"Of course," he answers honestly.

"Alright, I suppose I can play your fiancé for a couple hours," I say exasperatedly.

"Good," Shawn responds simply.

The two of us arrive at the apartment within twenty minutes. It's actually not too far from my parents or Teresa's house, so I guess that's good and bad. Good because I'll still be near Teresa, but bad because that means that my mom will randomly drop by. As I step out of the car, Shawn grabs my hand.

"We've got to play the part," he says with a wink.

As soon as we enter the lobby, I gasp in pleasure. It's the most elegant apartment building I've ever been in. There's security waiting at the desk to buzz us in. The lobby has been painted a deep maroon with cream accents. There are lush plants everywhere and rich leather couches to lounge on.

"Um, Shawn, I don't know if I can afford this place," I say uncertainly.

"Don't say no just yet," he responds, squeezing my hand.

We take the elevator up to the tenth floor and then take a right to apartment number 1041. This could be my future place, I think excitedly. Shawn knocks and an extremely muscular man promptly opens the door. He must live at the gym, I think, which is probably why he's putting this place up for rent. I accidentally laugh out loud at my own lame joke and then quickly cover my mouth.

"What's funny?" asks muscular man.

Maybe I should rename him sleazy man, I think, as I notice his eyes slowly travelling up and down my body. I have to stop myself from reaching up and slapping him across the face.

"This is Mark," Shawn introduces me. I can feel Shawn's arm wrap protectively around my shoulders and I see him give me an apologetic look. The reason he told this guy I was his fiancée is now completely clear to me.

"Hi Mark," I say politely.

"You must be the beautiful Jackie," he says, giving me a toothy grin.

"Yeah, that's me," I say. I wish that he would stop staring. It's really starting to creep me out.

"So, why don't you show Jackie the place," says Shawn, sensing my uneasiness.

"Sure, come on in," Mark moves aside.

Upon walking in, I instantly fall in love with the apartment. It's a corner condo, so it's bigger than the others in the building. There's hardwood floors, a huge balcony which wraps around the corner, spotlighting, a spacious living and dining room, a kitchen with all five appliances, one bedroom which is as big as the living room itself, a walk in closet, and a bathroom complete with a standing shower and Jacuzzi bathtub.

I look at Shawn, my eyes sparkling with joy. Then I turn to Mark, who's been lingering behind us the entire tour.

"How much?" I blurt out.

"Well, any friend of Shawn's is a friend of mine," starts Mark, licking his lips.

"Fiancée," I remind him.

"Right," responds Mark quickly. "Anyway, I'm sure that we can work something out. I need to rent it out rather quickly. As long as you're happy with the place."

"Well, I'm definitely happy," I respond.

"Great, why don't we all have a drink and we can work out the legal stuff then?" says Mark, sauntering towards the kitchen and pouring three glasses of scotch.

I accept my glass, have a seat on the couch and before I know it, we've sorted out all the details and Shawn and I are leaving the building. I'm going to be moving in late next week and couldn't be more pleased. I can't believe that Mark was able to give me such a good deal! And I feel even more grateful towards Shawn, without whom I would've never seen the place.

"Thanks so much Shawn," I say once we approach his car. "I honestly can't believe that Mark gave it to me for the same amount of rent that I'd be paying for a ratty basement apartment. He must be desperate to rent it out or something. The apartment is spectacular and I couldn't have found it without you."

"No problem," he says with a smile. "I'm so sorry that Mark acted like such a jerk though. I've noticed from the few times that I've met him that he does tend to come on strongly."

"So how do you know him anyway?" I ask Shawn.

"He's one of the client's I've had to deal with. What we call a high roller because he's got enough money to make my company do whatever he asks," Shawn responds opening the car door for me.

"Well, as long as I only have to deal with him once a month to give him my rent cheque, I think I can handle him," I reassure Shawn.

"Let me know if anything. I'll put him in his place," he replies, standing up a little straighter.

I laugh and punch him in the arm lightly. Shawn rubs his arm and gives me a pained expression, pretending that it actually hurt. Then we get in the car and drive off.

I can feel myself getting more and more excited as the weekend arrives. It feels like it's been forever since I've gone out with my friends, so this Saturday night is our night out on the town. Julie and Christian, along with his new boyfriend who happens to be the same guy he met at Devil's, are going to be coming with Teresa and me. The plan is to hit as many clubs and bars as possible, and then end the night with a trip to Denny's.

When I arrive at the club with Teresa by my side, we are given VIP treatment and are ushered in, skipping the long line-up. Julie has known the owner forever and we've come to be friendly with him too. He calls the three of us his Charlie's Angels. I always joke that I'm Jacqueline Smith. Aside from having the same name, I think we could practically be twins. Julie always rolls her eyes when she hears this.

We spot Julie and Christian at the bar. Christian is hanging all over his new boy toy, whom he introduces as Owen. Owen gives both of our hands a quick kiss, then he turns back to Christian and the two of them wrap themselves in a heated embrace. I can tell that this is going to be a night where I'll probably have to pry them off of each other to avoid hurling. I catch Teresa's eye and she must be thinking the same thing because she pretends to gag.

Julie, Teresa and I head to the dance floor to start the night off in style. Before long, three guys approach us and buy us drinks. We talk to them for a few minutes, then decide it's time to head over to the next club. We can't find Christian or Owen; so we ditch them and leave a message on Christian's phone to let him know.

The next club is so packed that I can barely breathe. We hang out for about ten minutes and then decide that the best thing to do is leave, unless we want to be groped in every way possible. The club where we end up after the overly crowded one is the worst yet. The people here are so grimy. I can see a couple doing something very

R-rated in the corner, and there are two girls dancing on stage, wearing almost nothing, and gyrating against each other. My jaw drops in surprise. Never, in all of my six-plus years of partying have I ever seen people engage in such disgusting behaviour. The three of us run out of the place practically screaming.

We enter the fourth club, expecting the worst and we decide that if this one is bad, we'll just head back to the first place where Julie knows the owner. But we are pleased to see that this one looks pretty good. Actually, it looks better than good. The walls are made of glass and have water flowing through them, and there are ornate decorations hanging from the ceiling. It's spacious and there are many people on the inside, yet it's still not packed. Also, the crowd looks very mature and classy, and the DJ is spinning the craziest songs. We nod at each other and head to the bar to order drinks.

After four shots of vodka straight up, I can feel my head starting to spin. I wasn't planning on getting drunk tonight, but I guess that it's a bit too late to change my mind now. Teresa is laughing at a story that Julie is recounting; something about how she was supposed to go into work today, but then she called her manager and told him that her dog died. I laugh stupidly along with Teresa and practically fall off my chair. The thought that I must look really idiotic vaguely crosses my mind, but is quickly pushed aside when I see a tall, broad-shouldered man with sandy-brown hair approach us. I recognize him at once and try to whisper a warning to Julie, but I can't seem to get the words out in time.

"Jules, I've missed you so much," he tells Julie, putting his arm around her shoulder.

Julie looks from him, to Teresa, then to me in alarm. Shoot, if my tongue didn't feel so numb, I could've warned her earlier.

"Vince, what're you doing here?" she asks, trying to make her voice sound calm.

Julie and Vince, who was formerly known as "Vincent" before he decided that it made him sound like one of those old guys who smoke pipes, used to date months ago. Apparently, they met at some high-society party that Julie had snuck into. He owned a bunch of hotels across the country and they started talking after they both had reached for the last hors d'oeuvres. One day she walked in and found him sitting on the deck of his mansion, clipping his toenails and it totally freaked her out how comfortable they'd gotten with each other. She dumped him straight away. Did I mention that Julie has major commitment issues? Poor Vince has never been able to get over it. Personally, I think that it's because he's so suave and wealthy. He's not used to girls saying no to him. When Julie told him to take a hike, it was a huge blow to his ego. Now, whenever we randomly bump into him, he turns into this needy, clingy guy, which totally goes against his persona. I can tell we're in for another scene as I see him begin to beg her back.

"I was hoping I'd run into you. Why'd you leave me Jules?" he questions her, looking so sad and desperate.

"God, we've been over this a hundred times!" Julie exclaims. "Please don't make yourself look so pathetic."

"But I know we can make it work," he pleads.

"No, we can't," Julie insists. "Why don't you try to date other people?"

"I've tried. No one makes me feel the way that you do," Vince says.

"Well then, you can't have been looking hard enough," Julie shakes her head.

"Can't we give it one more shot? Please? For old times sake?" Vince asks.

"Do you really think that having you continuously beg me like this is a turn-on or something," Julie asks, annoyed.

"I need you to know how much I care about you. I'd do anything. You would live like a queen," Vince offers.

Julie looks to Teresa and me for help and I stand up, but feel dizzy and sit back down. Teresa is going to have to handle this because the vodka is currently handling me.

"Vince, how about you let it go right now," Teresa starts gently. "Think of it this way: if it's meant to be, it'll happen."

Vince looks around anxiously and notices a small crowd beginning to gather. "You'll regret this, Julie. One day soon you'll see what you're giving up, and you'll wish that you'd changed your mind. And by then, it might be too late," he shouts as he stumbles away.

Everyone always claims that "if it's meant to be, it'll happen." How much trust can we actually put in destiny, something that we've never even seen? Who even came up with the concept of leaving everything up to destiny or fate? Personally, I think that it's the people too lazy to make things happen for themselves that rely on the "if-it's-meant-to-be-it'll-happen" phrase. I prefer to believe in the "if-you-want-things-done- you-have-to-do-them-yourself" quote -- although, I do believe in karma, which I guess sort of twists into the concept of fate and destiny. Karma makes sense though. If you put good into the world, it'll come back to you full circle; and if you put out negative energy, it'll kick you in the ass. I like the thought that you have control over what happens to you. Everyone should stop committing sins and then the world would be a much more peaceful place to live because nothing bad would be coming back to you tenfold. Maybe that's just my wishful thinking -- or maybe I'm seriously deluded.

Sunday evening, I'm sitting in my parents' home, filling them in on my amazing week. I can't believe my good luck. In the span of a week, I was able to secure a job and an apartment. I guess it just goes to show that you can do anything if you put your mind to it, or if you're really desperate!

We're waiting for a couple of my aunts, uncles and cousins to come over. My parents decided to throw a small get-together to celebrate my newfound success. I can't wait to rub it all in Sonia's face. I don't have to wait long. Within minutes, I can hear her irritating voice from the front door. Her family is the first to arrive and I run to greet her parents sweetly, the same way that she is greeting mine. I actually do adore both of her parents. I mean, her dad is my mom's brother, after all. But I'm always extra nice to them because I'm sure that Sonia takes every chance she gets to make me look bad in front of them.

I'm about to close the door when I see another person holding it ajar. Bobby enters our house and I have to bite back my surprise. I should have known that she would bring him. It's her way of saying, "You might have a job, but you're still single."

"Hi, Bobby. How're you?" I ask him.

"I'm doing well, Jackie. Congratulations on everything! I knew you could do it," he responds politely, giving me a quick hug.

"Thank you," I say, feeling Sonia's eyes burning a hole in my back.

I usher him into the house, along with the rest of the family, and shoot daggers at Sonia when she gives me a fake smile.

Before long, our house is crammed with family members. Unfortunately Nalini's family was unable to make it. Everyone's stuffing their faces, since that is a must at most family gatherings. People only come to eat. First, there are deep-fried snacks and sweets served with tea. Then, before you can even finish with that, along comes dinner, which includes so much food that we always have leftovers for a week.

I'm helping myself to a *gulaab jaman*, when Bindu Auntie comes and wraps me in a tight hug.

"I knew you would do it," she claims. "I told you that you just needed to get out on your own."

Interesting how fast someone's story can change. A couple of weeks ago, Bindu Auntie was telling me how sorry she felt for me because I would have such a hard time making it on my own, and now that I've accomplished it, she claims she was standing by me all the time.

"I know," I agree. It's easier for me to go along with what she's saying. In our culture, talking back to an adult or disagreeing with them can make you look like too much of a rebel. The rest of the adults would probably come down on me like hungry hawks.

"Good girl," she continues, patting my head as if I were a child.

"Good girl," mimics Sonia once Bindu Auntie is out of earshot.

"Oh, shut up," I tell Sonia, rolling my eyes.

"So you have a job and a place," she continues, as if I hadn't spoken. "Thank God. For a while my parents were thinking of having you come and live with us."

My eyebrows shoot up in horror. For once, both of us are in agreement that this would have been a nightmare from hell.

"Yeah, my thoughts exactly," Sonia says, looking at the expression on my face.

"Well, we don't have to worry then," I say, hoping that she will just walk away and leave me alone.

Sonia laughs. "Knowing you, you'll probably screw up so badly that it could still happen."

"I will not," I say heatedly.

"Of course you will," Sonia says as if it's obvious. "You'll be fired or homeless within a week. Two, max."

"You wish," I shoot back, annoyed that I can't come up with something better to say. "If that happens, I'll do whatever you want," I blurt out.

"Really?" Sonia says smirking. "I like the sound of that. Why don't you put your money where your mouth is and make it a proper bet? If you do fail, like I know you will, then you have to do whatever I ask."

"Deal," I say, trying to sound nonchalant.

"I think I better go and make a list of things to torture you with," says Sonia, laughing evilly and sauntering away.

I let out a sigh of relief once she's gone -- before realising the true extent of what I've just done. Not only do I have to worry about succeeding at my job and paying my bills, but also about the slight chance that if it doesn't work out, I'll be like Sonia's personal slave. I gulp and tell myself that I will do well, no matter what, because the latter is what scares me the most.

The next day, I am on my way to begin my new job. I take extra care getting ready in the morning. My hair is pulled back into a sleek chignon, and I'm wearing a fitted green Guess dress shirt with black pants from Tristan. I even got a manicure and my eyebrows done yesterday. After all, first impressions are everything and even though I've met the big boss, I'm sure that I'll be meeting my other fellow co-workers. I can't have them thinking that I'm some sloppy girl who can't dress herself to save her life.

I can feel my nerves making me extra jumpy as I push open the doors and walk into the office. The receptionist from the other day, a mousy-looking young girl, glances coldly at me before returning to her computer screen. I interrupt whatever she's doing on her computer -- probably playing solitaire -- and introduce myself.

"Hi, I'm Jackie Malhotra. Today's my first day here," I say with a smile, hoping that she might actually return it. I'm disappointed to see that, instead of smiling, she looks annoyed.

"Congratulations," she says sarcastically, popping her gum.

I'm slightly taken aback. I guess she isn't someone that I'll be spending lunch hours with.

"Um," I continue, getting myself together. "Is Tom in? I believe he's supposed to show me what to do."

She reaches for the phone and pages Tom, and then she gives me a look, that tells me to step away from her desk. Seriously, what is her problem?

I wait patiently for Tom, and he arrives shortly after. "Jackie, you're on time," he exclaims, shaking my hand.

"Yes, of course," I say, trying to sound professional. I consider asking him what is wrong with his receptionist, when to my amazement, she smiles, stands up and introduces herself. Talk about doing a complete 180. She must be on some crazy medication or something. Maybe she steals it herself from the clinic's own stash.

"Hi Jackie, my name is Roz," she says sweetly, glancing at Tom.

I realise immediately what she's doing. She's sucking up to him! If she thinks that I'm the type of person who'll put up with this, she's wrong. In fact, she has no idea who she's dealing with. But for now, I have no choice but to act as if she isn't a two-faced loser.

"Nice to meet you, Roz," I respond.

"So, Jackie, let me introduce you to everyone else who works here," says Tom, leading me through the clinic.

After about twenty minutes, I've met the other two psychiatrists who work in the office: Melvin, a tall, skinny Chinese man, and Richard, an elderly man with kind eyes and white hair.

Then Tom shows me my desk, which seems a bit small to me, but I decide not to complain about it yet. He leaves me with a stack of papers to file. The filing takes the entire morning and before I know it, it's lunchtime.

So far, the job seems extremely boring, but I keep on telling myself that it's only the first day. Most first days are always like this, right? I think back to the last time I had a first day of work, and I decide that so far, this is definitely better than that day. That day, I was working in retail, at one of my favourite stores, Dynamite, and it turned out to be a day from hell. Not only was I twenty minutes late (I told my manager it was due to traffic, but in all honesty, I just had to stop for ice cream), but I also ended up having a customer complain (she claimed that I was too busy talking on the phone to help her) and I even ended up knocking down a whole display of new sweaters that had just arrived (I couldn't talk my way out of that one). Needless to say, I never went back.

Today is actually starting to sound fantastic compared to that day. I mean, I've lasted so far without any sort of disaster. I leave my desk for lunch, thinking that some greasy fast food sounds like an appropriate meal. I also decide that if Tom's not around, I might put Roz in her place. I'm lost in my thoughts when I bump into a tall, lean man. He turns around in surprise, and nothing could prepare me for the sight that meets my eyes.

"Ravi!" I exclaim in shock.

He looks back at me, equally shocked. "Jackie?" he asks, as if he thinks his eyes are deceiving him as well.

"What're you doing here?" we both ask in unison.

"I work here," I respond at the same time as Ravi.

We both stop, almost afraid to go on.

"What do you mean, you work here?" I ask, thinking that I must not have heard him correctly.

At that moment, Tom walks through the hall. "Oh, I see that you've met Ravi," he says cheerily. "He's another psychiatrist who works here. I knew I'd forgotten to introduce you to someone."

I glace dumbfounded from Tom to Ravi. Surely, this must be a joke.

"Ravi, this is Jackie. She's our new office assistant," continues Tom.

I catch Ravi's eye, and I don't know who's more perturbed- him or me.

"Well, I've got to get back to my patient," says Tom, giving us both a pat on our shoulders and then walking away.

"I, I thought you were a doctor?" I say stupidly.

"I am. A psychiatrist is also considered a doctor to most people," says Ravi, as if he's talking to a five-year-old.

"I know that," I snap, annoyed at his tone, "but the way your parents were going on about it, it's as if you were a brain surgeon or something."

"Don't talk about my parents like they're liars," says Ravi, an edge entering his voice.

I roll my eyes. "Whatever. Look, if we both must work here, let's at least try to make it painless, okay?"

"Agreed. Just stay out of my way and I'm sure things will be fine," he says.

"Trust me, I have no desire to cross paths with you," I shoot back.

And with that, we both give each other a final look and continue on our separate ways.

This all goes back to karma, I know it. It can't just have been some sort of coincidence. I'm sure that I've done something in the past that caused Ravi and I to end up working at the same clinic. I mean, what are the chances? In all the places for me to find a job, I have to get one at the exact same place where he's a psychiatrist. What could I have possibly done for karma to come and kick me in the ass like this? Perhaps it's because of that one time that I stole a pair of earrings when I was thirteen. Or maybe it's because of that time that I threw a secret party when my parents went away and that one kid broke my mom's vase. My mom freaked out and I miraculously managed to convince her that she herself had broken it years ago. Or no, I figured it out. It definitely has got to be because of that time that I...actually maybe that's not a story that I should be retelling. Now that I think about, there's quite a bit of stuff that karma could be getting me back for. I'm sort of surprised that all it's thrown my way so far is having to work with Ravi. Then again, maybe I shouldn't speak so soon.

Email Messages:

Dear Jackie Malhotra:
I have reviewed your resume and based upon your qualifications, I would like to schedule an interview. Please email or call me at your earliest convenience.

Kelly Trimble
Human Resources
Make-Me-Over Boutique

Dear Jackie,
I understand that you are looking for employment. Our client, a distributor of

electronics, is holding an open house this weekend to hire for several different positions. If you are interested in attending, please email me and I will forward you further information.

Larry Fischer
L.F. Employment Services

Go figure that the minute I find a job, I have all these other offers coming in as well. Where were all of these interviews two or three weeks ago when I was desperate? Well, it's too late for them now. They should be very sorry that they lost the chance for a superb employee like me to work with them. Instead, it's lucky Tom who plucked me up as soon as he had the chance. And so far, working at the clinic has proven to be great! Okay, great I guess is a little bit of an exaggeration. Maybe boring is more accurate. Yes, definitely boring. All he's made me do so far is filing. Apparently no one there has filed in years. There are boxes and boxes of filing to be done. I'm only at year 2001 right now, and at this rate, I'll be filing until next year. My poor fingers are all scraped with paper cuts. It doesn't help that I continuously bump into that arrogant jerk, Ravi. He makes it a point to saunter by when I'm on my hands and knees, struggling to stick a file in the right drawer. Then he always mutters some sort of sarcastic comment. His favourite is something along the lines of, "What's a

Government official doing here, filing? Wait, this must be a top-secret assignment, right?"

I could kill him for making me feel so small. At first I would shoot back comments, but that just seemed to provoke him more. Now I've decided that a better tactic is to bite my tongue. So far, it's worked because yesterday he ignored me completely.

It amazes me to think how different people can be. On the one hand, I have to deal with loser Ravi, and then on the other hand, there's Shawn. He's so amazing. Things are flowing smoothly between the two of us. We talk to each other on a daily basis, and last weekend he even helped me move into my fabulous new apartment. This is probably the longest relationship I've had where things have gone so wonderfully. And I know that that should make me a little wary, but I just can't help it. Maybe there are perfect guys out there. Maybe there is such a thing as a relationship without flaws. And maybe, just maybe, I was lucky enough to find it.

Monday is by far, the worst day of the week. It's the beginning of the work week, everyone seems so depressed and tired, and for some strange reason, I've noticed how the weather is always terrible.

This particular Monday also signifies the beginning of my second official week of work at the clinic. Unfortunately, I've managed to sleep in and am running twenty minutes behind schedule. I decide to stop at Tim Horton's on the way, I mean, if I'm already late, what's another ten minutes? I grab an extra coffee for Tom, to butter him up and help him forget all about the fact that I'm late.

I arrive at the clinic, and put on an extra sweet smile when I see Roz sitting behind her desk, glaring at me. If she weren't so mean, I'd probably help her out and give her a makeover or something. Her hair is always slightly greasy, and her skin is super dry. What she needs is a good facial and hair treatment. Plus, she's thin, and yet, instead of wearing nice, fitted clothing, she always wears stuff that is two sizes too big. Sometimes I almost feel sorry for her. Maybe she's rude because she's so unhappy with herself. And then, when I see her still glaring at me, I change my mind quickly and go back to thinking she's just a slimy two-faced sneak.

"You're late," she says coldly.

"I know," I answer simply. "Where's Tom?"

"He's with a patient, working, which is probably something you could be doing as well," she says. Then the phone rings, and she turns to answer it.

I continue on my way to my desk and then settle in for another long day of filing. About twenty minutes later, as I'm sorting through the F's and G's, I see Tom standing in front of me, looking stern. I gulp, and think that this can't be good.

"Hi Tom," I say lightly.

"Good morning Jackie, or it could practically be afternoon considering the time you came in," he responds.

"I know, I'm sorry I was late," I apologise. "I brought you coffee!" I exclaim suddenly remembering the plan.

Tom glances quickly at the coffee and I notice that his eyes soften slightly. "Thank you, but I still have to reprimand you. I like you Jackie. I think you've got a certain spunk that could turn this clinic into a fun place to work. But tardiness is not something that I take lightly," he finishes.

"Okay," I nod. I realise that at this point, I should take the same approach that I do with my relatives and just agree with him. It always seems to get people off my back. "You're right. It won't happen again."

"Great," he says. He picks up his coffee and turns to leave. I can't help but smile. It never fails.

Much later, I'm stretching my fingers and decide to take a quick break. I pick up my glass and saunter towards the water cooler, which is located at the very back of the clinic. I've suggested to Tom that it should be moved to the front so that the patients are able to access it as well. Plus, it won't be so far for me to get to either. I think he's going to seriously consider it. I see Richard come up and stand beside me, water cup in hand.

"Hello Richard," I greet him.

"Good day to you Jacqueline," responds Richard politely in his British accent.

I absolutely adore the way that Richard speaks, especially when he calls me Jacqueline. I haven't bothered to correct him by telling him that that's not technically my name. I have a feeling that Janaki just wouldn't sound as pretty. Richard always sounds so cultured. Apparently he moved here from England only five years ago and secured a job at the clinic right away. His wife had just passed away and he'd decided that he needed a change of scenery. So far, he's told me that he loves living in Toronto, although he misses the beautiful architecture that makes up his old hometown, Manchester. Richard gives me a quick nod once his glass is filled and then heads back towards his office.

I decide to take a walk around the clinic to give my legs some exercise. I head in the opposite direction of my desk. The few times that I've wandered aimlessly around the clinic before, I've come to notice how big it actually is. Aside from all four of the doctor's having their own offices, there's the reception area, a huge storage room filled with filing cabinets (which is where I've been spending the majority of my time), a kitchen, a washroom, and even a living room type area. Plus there's also the small area near the storage room, which is where my desk is situated.

At the moment, my legs carry me in the opposite direction of my desk; towards the kitchen and then I freeze in shock.

Standing not even ten feet in front of me are Ravi and Roz, wrapped in a passionate embrace. They both must have heard me approaching because they spring apart as if they've been electrocuted and then look at me shamefully. I can't help but keep my feet rooted for a second. Then all of our cheeks flame in embarrassment.

"Err, I'll just be going," I mumble before taking a step back.

"Uh, wait," starts Ravi. Roz looks at him questioningly. "You aren't going to um, tell anyone about this, are you?" he asks.

"What, that you're a cheating dog?" I ask, my brain finally starting to grasp the situation.

"What?" asks Ravi in confusion.

"You told me you had some long time girlfriend," I answer back.

"I do," states Ravi. "Jackie, meet Roz, my girlfriend."

I look at the two of them, trying to see if they're kidding.

"This is who you were talking about?" I ask, trying to mask my surprise.

"Yes," he admits.

"So why are you acting as if you've been caught in the act?" I ask suspiciously.

"Because, employees aren't allowed to date other employees," Roz says finally.

"I see," I nod. "Well, then just a little suggestion. Try to refrain from sucking face at the office." With that I turn and walk away.

I can only remember a few times in my life where I was in the wrong place at the wrong time. Once, I walked in on an old boyfriend of mine, Kam (the student teacher), while he was trying on one of my bras. Needless to say, I screamed in shock and was so freaked out that I dumped him on the spot. I couldn't even listen to his explanations, but he went on about how he just wanted to see what it felt like. I recently heard that he is now seeking psychiatric help. I'd definitely say that with the Ravi situation, it's another time where I was in the wrong place at the wrong time. I would love to go back in time and never have witnessed Ravi and Roz all over each other like that. I don't really know why it bothers me so much. I should be enjoying the fact that I've got some dirt on Ravi, and instead, I can't get the image of what I saw out of my head. Maybe I'm becoming a nicer person or something, because right now I don't even feel like using the information against Ravi. Or maybe I'm losing my mind.

During dinner that night with Shawn, I'm totally out of it. And I can tell that he's noticed because every time he asks me a question, I either say something that makes absolutely no sense, or then I stare at him blankly.

"Okay, what's up?" Shawn asks finally.

"Nothing," I respond a little too quickly.

"It doesn't sound like nothing," starts Shawn. "You know you can talk to me, right?"

Yeah, like I can tell him that what's bothering me is the fact that I saw two of my co-workers kissing. I don't even know why it's been on my mind. He'll probably just laugh and say something like maybe we should give them both a run for their money.

"No, seriously, it's nothing. Trust me," I insist.

"Okay," he says, while I silently beg him to change the topic. "So, I've been thinking. I know it might sound like it's too soon," Shawn says looking quite nervous all of a sudden.

Oh no, I think frantically. He's going to say we should move in together, or that we should get engaged! I'm not ready for that. We've only been dating a few weeks. How can he already expect something so huge from me? I glance down at my glass of champagne, almost expecting to see a diamond ring sitting at the bottom. I knew this was too good to be true. He must be insane.

"Shawn, wait," I interrupt him.

"No, no, let me finish," he continues. "I have to go away on business for the weekend, and I was wondering if you'd like to come with me."

I stare at him a moment, at a loss for words. This is probably the last thing I was expecting because of his serious tone. Then I breathe a huge sigh of relief, telling myself that he isn't insane after all.

"Wow," I start.

"It's okay if you don't want to. I understand," Shawn says looking slightly let down.

"Actually, no, I would really like that," I tell him, reaching over and grabbing his hand. "Where are we going?"

"Montreal," he says returning my smile.

"Montreal!" I exclaim in delight. "I love that city!"

"Well, I'm glad to hear it," he says with a laugh.

I nod excitedly. This is actually a really good step in our relationship, I think. We'll get to know each other even better, while spending the weekend in one of the most beautiful cities in Canada. I can't wait until the weekend arrives.

The next few days at work are spent with me filing as usual and also avoiding Ravi and Roz, which is really hard since I've come to realise that the clinic is not as big as I'd originally thought.

By the end of the week, I'm exhausted. I'm grabbing my purse and getting ready to head home and prepare myself for a much deserved weekend getaway, when I see Ravi walking towards my desk. He clears his throat and looks at me.

"Hi," he starts. "Look, I know that we've been avoiding each other because of ah, the incident."

"Yes, and it suits me just fine," I tell him matter-of-factly.

"Yeah, well, I just wanted to tell you..." he trails off and I notice a look on his face that I've never seen before. Wait, is he going to thank me, I wonder, and his next words confirm my belief. "I just wanted to thank you for not giving away our secret," he finishes.

I nod. I've never before seen him look so sincere and honest. He actually looks like he could be a nice guy. Then the way that he's tormented me since I first met him enters my mind and pushes away all other thoughts.

"Yeah, well don't think that I won't in the future," I say with a hint of warning.

Ravi looks at me in alarm. "Are you trying to blackmail me?"

"No," I say quickly. I actually hadn't meant it to come out like that. "I'm just telling you to be careful and that if I have to see any more grotesque displays of public affection in the work place then I'll have no choice but to tell Tom."

"Really," says Ravi and I can see all hints of sincerity gone from his face. "Well if I didn't know any better, I'd say you were jealous."

His statement catches me totally off guard. "Jealous?" I spit at him. "Are you kidding me? I'll have you know that I'm in a serious, meaningful relationship right now with the perfect guy. In fact, we're going away together this weekend," I add as an after thought.

"Wow, I believe that almost as much as I believe that you do actually work for the FBI," Ravi says sarcastically.

"How dare you," I seethe.

We glare at each other a moment longer and then I see him turn and walk away. I'm left knowing that my first instincts were correct with this guy. He's nothing more than an egotistical, annoying jerk. And what he does with his personal life is something that I'm sure will be found out sooner or later, without me having to mention a word.

I open the door to my wonderful apartment and am left in awe as usual. It's been almost a week and I still can't get over the fact that I actually live here.

I'm looking forward to when I can entertain guests and throw lavish parties. I'd make them like the kind you see in those old movies. Everyone would come dressed in formal attire, and I'd have waiters serving cocktails and hors d'oeuvres. I'd be wandering around, schmoozing with all of the rich people that stop in and they'd be telling me what a spectacular party I've thrown. Of course I'd be looking fabulous, probably wearing an original Vera Wang. Perhaps Vera herself would stop by and everyone would be able to see how much I've accomplished in such a short time. I decide to start looking for the perfect party dress as soon as possible.

But for the time being, I've got some time to kill. It's only five and Shawn isn't coming to pick me up until nine. Then we're taking a late flight and should be in Montreal by one in the morning.

I realise that I'm starving and wander over to my kitchen to pour a bowl of cereal. Unfortunately it's one of the only things that I know how to prepare. I tried to make pasta the other day and let's just say that it was lucky I managed to get the situation under control before I had to call the fire department. I've made a note to pick up a cook book and watch more cooking shows so that one day soon I can make a decent meal. I'm getting really sick of cereal and fast food.

When I've finished my bowl of Froot Loops, I wander into my bedroom and flop lazily onto my bed, switching on the TV. Then I notice a pile of clothing lying in the corner. It looks menacing because of the way it's taking up more and more of my floor space every single day.

I groan and come to terms with the fact that I should probably do my laundry, at least until I'm able to afford so many clothes that I can just wear them once and toss them. I get up grudgingly and throw the lot into a basket. Then I make my way to the washer and dryer, which I accidentally stumbled upon on a late night trip to the washroom. I had no idea that I even owned a washer and dryer and always figured that the closet by the washroom was extra storage space. So you can imagine my surprise when I opened it up and saw the two appliances staring me in the face.

I've never done my own laundry before, but I can't see it being that hard. I mean I should just be able to throw the clothes into the washer and hit the start button right? I'm thinking about how this should be a piece of cake as I empty all of my clothes into the washing machine. Then I close the lid and stare at the dials. I feel panic start to creep into me when I see how many different options there are. There's a setting for delicate, cotton, or wool. There's another setting for black, white or colour. I also notice a little switch that says hot, warm or cold. And there's yet another one that says low, medium, or high.

I open the lid and then stare at the clothes lying inside. Maybe I'm supposed to separate them, but if I separate them into the according categories by colour and setting, then there's only about two or three that could fit into each. The company that made this machine cannot possibly expect me to waste a whole load of water on just a couple of pieces of clothing, can they? And wouldn't it take me forever to finish washing everything if I did it that way? No, they must be trying to pull a fast one on me. I'm sure that I'm just supposed to do them all at the same time and pick the setting which fits most of the clothes. I congratulate myself on my quick thinking. Then I glance down at the clothes again so I can set the dials.

First, I guess most of my clothing is cotton, so I twist the dial towards that setting. Many of my clothes are also full of vibrant colour, so that setting is not a thinker. The hot, warm or cold switch throws me for a minute before I decide they must be talking about what type of weather the clothing is worn in. Well, it's late summer, so it's still pretty warm. And lastly, I am dumbstruck when thinking about the low, medium and high switch. I close my eyes and flip it randomly, thinking that if I've gotten the other three settings correct, the last one probably doesn't matter as much.

It strikes me then that I've forgotten something. The soap! I giggle to myself. It would have been really stupid of me to forget that. Luckily I picked up some laundry detergent at the grocery store the other day. I shudder as I remember how that trip went. I had to ask one of the employees to help me find everything that I needed, because I had no idea how to make my way around the store. There are so many options. How am I supposed to know whether I should get seedless cucumbers or not? Or whether I prefer dishwashing liquid with or without aloe vera? By the end of the three hours, the poor stock room boy looked exhausted.

I ended up tipping him. Then the manager came to find out and was pissed because according to her, it wasn't the boy's job to become my personal shopper. I just glared at the woman and told her not to expect my business there again. How rude!

I pour in some detergent and watch it turn to foam as the water hits it. Hmm...it doesn't look as if the cupful of soap I just added is going to be enough. I glance at the label on the bottle and am disappointed to see that it doesn't state exactly how much detergent I need. I shrug and pour in another cupful. Then I close the lid, feeling a deep sense of satisfaction. I guess it's not that hard after all.

Much later, I'm lying on my bed, intrigued by the current episode of *Sex and the City* that is airing on TV. I was surprised to find that it's an episode I've never seen before. I've already packed my bag for the weekend, or actually I should say bags because I ended up having to pack three. I'm hoping that it's not too much of an issue. I tried my hardest to narrow it down, but then I noticed that everything that I was packing was an absolute necessity. After all, what if it rains and I need a pair of close-toed shoes instead of the three pairs of sandals that I'm taking? And what if there's a cold front and I need a sweater to wear on top of a tank top? Then I realised that I obviously couldn't just take the one sweater or the one pair of shoes, because what if it rained or was cold all weekend? I checked the weather and was pleased to see that the forecast is supposed to be warm and sunny, but still, the weather channel has been wrong before. And I can't imagine how distraught I'd be without the proper attire.

I hear my buzzer and then I rush to let the person in, thinking that it must be Shawn. I'm surprised to find that it's my parents. Shoot, what're they doing here? They cannot know that I'm going away for the weekend with Shawn. It'll definitely change their mind about what a good, decent Indian girl I am. In their minds, going out clubbing with friends is okay, getting drunk is bad. Talking to boys and going out on casual dates with them is okay, going and spending a whole weekend unsupervised with one is bad.

"Hi mom, dad," I greet them. "This is a nice surprise."

"Hello *beta*," responds dad. "We came to visit your new apartment. We thought that you have had enough time to set up everything by now."

"Oh, yes of course," I reply, glancing at the clock on the wall.

I have about twenty minutes to get them out of here before Shawn gets here. I take them on a quick tour of the condo and then pray that they have somewhere else to be. Although I'm pleased about their visit since it shows that they do care and are supporting me, I'm also wishing that they'd chosen another time.

"Aren't you going to offer us some *chai*, coffee?" asks mom. "Here, let me make it."

She walks purposely towards the kitchen and then starts rummaging through my cabinets. "*Chee, beta*, you have nothing proper to eat in the kitchen. I will have to bring you food next time I come."

"Um, yes mom. I miss your cooking," I agree with her, still glancing at the clock from the corner of my eye. I've got ten minutes. Now I begin to pray that Shawn will be late.

"You seem nervous," dad states.

"Me, nervous?" I ask. "Of course not. I was actually just on my way out."

"Oh? Where were you going?" asks mom from the kitchen.

"Uh, grocery shopping," I say, relieved that my mom can't see my expression so she can't know that I'm lying.

"Oh, we will come with you," mom says excitedly, as she comes back into the living room. "I need to get a few things too."

"Um, no mom, you guys can't," I blurt out suddenly, trying to come up with an excuse.

"Why not?" asks mom suspiciously.

I can tell that she's trying to read my mind, so I block out all indecent thoughts of spending the weekend alone with Shawn. I frantically try to think of a logical excuse.

"Oh, shoot, sorry did I say I needed to go grocery shopping? I actually meant that I was on my way to Teresa's," I finish lamely.

Mom gives me a quizzical look and I know that she's not buying it. But by a dash of good luck, she shrugs and decides not to badger me like she normally would've.

"Okay, we will be on our way then," she says. "But you owe your Papa and me a good cup of *chai* next time."

I breathe a sigh of relief and bid them both goodbye. Then I collapse on my couch and am thankful that my parents left when they did. I can't imagine them meeting Shawn in this sort of way. It'd be a cheerful encounter. I can imagine it now. "Hello, mom, dad, this is the man that I've been secretly seeing out of wedlock and I am planning on going away with him for a whole weekend."

I think my parents would tie me up and drag me back home, cursing about how I've been on my own for a couple of weeks and have already become so corrupted. Then they'd lock me in my room and refuse to let me out until I agreed to get married.

Within minutes I hear my buzzer once again. I rush to let Shawn in. He gives me a quick kiss and asks if I'm ready.

"Of course I'm ready," I tell him. "As if I'm ever late."

"You and late? The two don't go in the same sentence," he rolls his eyes. "So where's your bag?"

"Right in my room," I respond. "I'm just going to grab my purse."

I walk towards my living room while Shawn goes into my bedroom to retrieve my bags.

"Jackie, how much stuff are you actually taking?" he calls in astonishment.

"Just the bare necessities," I respond casually.

I meet him at the front door and laugh out loud. He's managed to carry out all three bags at once and is shuddering under the weight.

"Let me help," I offer, taking the smallest and lightest bag.

"Thanks," he says, shaking his head. "You do realise that we'll only be gone for two days, right?"

"Yep," I respond, giving him a sweet smile.

Shawn shrugs. "Okay, I hope the plane is big enough to fit your entire wardrobe," he jokes.

"You think it won't be?" I ask worriedly.

I see him laugh and slap him playfully on the shoulder. Then we walk out of my apartment. I lock the door behind me and smile to myself, thinking about how much fun we're going to have together.

Okay, so I'm not the best flyer. In fact, I'm probably one of the worst. I hate flying, but I love to travel. How ironic is that? The last time that I travelled by plane, I was a nervous wreck. I was going to Mexico with Teresa. The flight was about five hours long, and I spent about four and half freaking out. Teresa had to hold my hand the entire time. When she got up to go to the washroom, I had the flight attendant sit in her place. I don't think I've ever seen someone as relieved as he was when Teresa came back. I've heard that you're more likely to die in a car accident, than on a plane. You'd think that this statistic would help and make it easier for me to fly, but it doesn't. I guess it's just because I'm used to travelling by car. I think it's also the thought of being stuck thousands of feet in the air with no escape. If a plane goes down, your best bet is to jump out the window with a parachute (which to me might as well be a flimsy cloth) tied to your back. Are you kidding me? I might as well plunge to my death. If a car crashes, at least my body is still on solid ground. I wish there was an easier way to travel. I wish I could just say out loud where I wanted to go and 'pop', two seconds later I was there. Think about how much money, time and stress that would save! Perhaps in like a hundred years, it will be possible. It's too bad that I'm living in the present and not a hundred years in the future.

Text Messages:
Sender: Teresa
Sent: 2:00am
Hey babe, hope ur havin a blast in Montreal. Call me wen u get bak. Dont do anytin I wudnt do!

Sender: Julie
Sent: 3:46am
OMG! Im so drunk. Cant believe u went 2 Montreal w/o me. Make sure u get some action ;)

By the time Shawn and I arrive in Montreal, we're both too tired to do anything other than hit the sack. I feel exhausted from my nerves on the plane and Shawn's exhausted from having to continuously calm me down and tell me that we weren't going to crash. I almost feel sorry for him. I bet he'll never want to fly with me again! Too bad for him we've still got the return trip to worry about.

The next morning I get up and find myself in an empty hotel room. I look around and immediately start to wonder if I imagined coming to Montreal with Shawn. Maybe Shawn's a hallucination and doesn't exist at all. There's this woman who comes into the clinic, Janette, and she's being treated for mild schizophrenia. She claims that her twin sister, Jennifer, is trying to ruin her life. In reality, Janette and Jennifer are one and the same.

But now as I lay alone in the hotel bed, I wonder if something like that is contagious. What if Shawn isn't real, and I totally made him up?

The phone rings, bringing me out of my thoughts. "Hello?" I answer.

"Hey Jackie," I hear Shawn's chipper voice. "Sorry to leave without waking you, but you looked too sweet to disturb."

I smile to myself. There's no way that I could make up someone who could talk to me like that.

"Anyway," Shawn continues. "I'm going to be at this meeting for a couple more hours, but I should be back by the time you're ready. Then, the rest of the day and night is ours."

"Sounds like a plan," I tell him, still smiling.

"Good. Order room service, but don't eat too much because we've got dinner reservations."

"Room service?" I ask, temporarily surprised. I've never had anyone offer to let me order room service before. One time, Danny and I stayed at a hotel, and he actually forbid me to order it because according to him, it's too expensive. Now that I think about it, I actually remember him telling me to take as many 'complimentary' items as I could, including toilet paper, towels, and the light bulbs in the lamps.

Shawn laughs. "Yes, room service. The company pays for it though, so don't get any bright ideas."

"Don't tempt me," I joke back. "Alright, so I guess that I'll see you soon."

We say our goodbyes and hang up. Then I lie back in bed and curl up under the covers. If he's going to be another couple hours, I've got plenty of time to get some more sleep.

The door opens, which wakes me up immediately. I see Shawn enter the room and I jolt up in bed.

"Oh no!" I exclaim. "What time is it?"

Shawn looks at me in surprise. "You're still sleeping? It's almost three!"

"I'm not even ready yet!" I exclaim.

"And how long is that going to take?" Shawn asks me, raising his eyebrows.

"I don't know!" I snap. "Don't rush me." The look on his face makes me calm down. "I'm sorry, I'm just not a morning person."

"It's almost evening!" Shawn says, throwing up his hands.

"Ugh, you know what I mean," I say, tossing off the covers.

"I can't believe you're still asleep! I called you like three hours ago and I thought that that was late enough," he says in an exasperated tone

I grab my bag, say nothing to him, and head for the washroom.

It takes me over an hour to get ready, and the whole time I can see Shawn sitting in front of his laptop, looking at me from over the screen. We don't speak. I think I might have annoyed him. But it's not really my fault that I slept in. He should have called me when he was almost done.

I apply a last coat of mascara, then go and stand beside Shawn. I'm hoping that he'll break the silence first by telling me how fabulous I look. I'm disappointed to find that he ignores me and continues typing on his computer.

"Hi, I'm ready," I announce.

"Great, the tour that I had planned for us to go on left a half hour ago," he says sarcastically.

"Then why don't we do something else," I suggest.

"Dinner reservations aren't for another three hours," he responds, not glancing up from his screen.

"Look, what are you so upset about?" I ask with an edge in my voice. "So I slept in, it's not the end of the world."

Shawn finally turns to look at me. I can tell that he's considering what I just said. Then his eyes soften. "I know, you're right."

I give him an 'I told you so' look and stand with my arms crossed. "I don't get why you got so upset about it."

"I know, that's not really my style to get so worked up," he agrees. "I guess it's just because I am a morning person. The fact that you slept so late sort of freaked me out. And I had all this stuff planned for us to do. I hate not being on schedule," he admits reluctantly.

"Wow, you need to loosen up," I tell him, rubbing his shoulders. "And I think I'm just the right person to help you with that."

Shawn looks at me questioningly. I grab his hand and pull him towards the door.

"Wait, let me just finish what I was typing," he protests.

"Later," I tell him. "We've got the whole day and night to do what we want. And you can forget about the dinner reservations, because as of right now, everything that's been planned is out the window. It's time to be spontaneous."

The next two days pass by in a blur of fun. Shawn finally relaxes; in fact, he almost misses an important meeting because I'm teaching him how to roller-skate. Can you believe that he's never been roller-skating before? I don't know how he managed anything before I came along.

On Sunday night, when he finally drops me off at my apartment, I'm left in a content mood. However, it's not an emotion that lasts for long.

I open the door to my apartment and for some reason I get a funny feeling. It's almost as if I've forgotten something. I immediately assume that it's got something to do with my luggage and panic. But upon looking down, I see that I've got all three bags with me. Then I think that maybe I've left behind my flat iron, so I rush to my bedroom and empty the contents of my bags onto the floor. I scatter through them and do a quick scan of everything. It all seems to be in order. Then I decide that I must be worrying about nothing and wander to the kitchen to make myself a cup of tea.

It's then that it hits me. My laundry! I put it all in to be washed before I left and never took it out to dry or fold!

I abandon my cup of tea and make my way to the washer, assuming that I'll probably just have to rewash the clothes. But when I open the lid, my jaw drops. My nose scrunches in disgust because it smells as if something's rotting. I pick up an article of clothing, and it only gets worse. What used to be my favourite cream Chanel halter is now my pink rag. The rest of the clothing has had the same sort of mutant transformation. Everything has shrunken, some are the wrong colour, and they all reek.

I cry out in frustration as I see the tag attached to the Chanel halter. It reads 'dry clean only' and as I stare at many of the other pieces of clothing, they have the same specific instructions plainly stated on their tags. My clothes! My beautiful clothes are ruined. There must be about $2000 worth of clothing in this demonic washing machine, and now they all look as if they're something you wash a car with.

How am I going to replace everything? I don't have that sort of money. Most of them were bought with my parent's credit cards. I can't possibly afford any of these things with my current salary.

The only bright side to any of this is that luckily, not all of my clothes are ruined. I only washed a portion of what I own. But then, as I look down at some of my favourite pieces, all wrinkled and damaged, I can't help but let a few tears fall.

I know that I've screwed up plenty of times before, but this time it's different because I was trying so hard. It's not just about the clothes. It's about the fact that I actually failed at something when I told myself that I would succeed no matter what. If Sonia could see me right now, she'd cackle evilly. This is exactly what she expected to happen, and I guess I just confirmed her beliefs. I feel like such a failure because this one incident proves that my world isn't a perfect place, as I'd originally started to believe it could be.

Much later that night, I've drunk a whole bottle of wine on my own, and am wallowing in sorrow. I hear my doorbell ring and I roll over on my couch, wishing that whoever it is will go away. But the person on the other side of the door turns out to be very persistent as I hear the bell ring again and again. Then the ringing turns to banging and I know that if I don't answer the door, my head is going to explode from all the noise.

"What?" I cry as I pull open the door.

"You never called to let me know you got home safe," says Teresa as she pushes her way into my condo. "I've been calling your phone like crazy, trying to make sure you're okay. I knew something was wrong," she continues, taking a look at my face. "Have you been drinking? Oh no, what happened?"

I turn away from her and make my way back to the couch. I pick up my almost empty bottle of wine and take the last sip.

"It's worse than I thought," she says worriedly. "You had a terrible time with Shawn? You found out he's a mama's boy? Your work called you to fire you? You're being thrown out of your fabulous new place?"

I finally look at her. "No, but thanks for pointing out everything else that could and probably will go wrong," I say sourly.

"Aw, Jackie," she says coming to sit beside me. "What happened then?"

"I ruined my clothes," I say sullenly. "They're complete garbage. I can't even wash a load of clothes without screwing up. I should've guessed this would happen."

"All of your clothes are ruined?" she asks sympathetically, putting her arm around my shoulders.

"No, but some of my favourite ones are," I respond.

"It's okay. This is a good thing," she says trying to make me feel better. "When you fall, you just have to get right back up and make things better. How else will you learn? You can't possibly have expected to do everything right from the start."

I look at her, but say nothing. Then I stand up, sway slightly on the spot and immediately slump back down onto the couch. I think I've drunk more than I can handle. The wine is starting to make me feel dizzy and sleepy.

"How much did you drink?" Teresa asks with a hint of concern.

"Not enough," I reply. This time, I force myself to concentrate as I stand up and make my way to the kitchen. I know I've got another bottle in the cupboard waiting for me.

Teresa must be able to read my mind, because she gets there before I do. "Well I think you've had enough," she insists, picking up the bottle and holding it away from me.

"Fine!" I say dejectedly. "That's just fine. I'll just continue to be a screw up my whole life then, shall I?"

"You're not going to be a screw up," Teresa replies. "The way I see it, you've done pretty damn well so far. You managed to get a job and a condo in like a week!"

I consider what she's saying, shrug then go back to the couch. I grab a blanket and cuddle up underneath it.

It must be ten minutes later, when all of a sudden I feel a giant tug on my blanket. "Get up," Teresa tells me sternly. "I can't stand to see you so down. We're going to fix this, don't worry."

I look at her questioningly. She's holding a cup of steaming liquid, which she forces into my hands.

"It's coffee. Drink it. It'll sober you up and give you energy. I've thrown out all of the destroyed clothes, which were still lying in the washing machine. Now you're going to get ready and we'll go to a movie or something," she says with a nod of her head.

I feel so touched, that I don't argue and instead take a sip of the coffee. Then I stand up and give Teresa a hug. "Thanks. I really don't know what I'd do without you," I tell her.

When I was sixteen, I'd moved to a new school. It was really tough, having to move and start all over again when you're in grade eleven. By that age, most kids know who their friends are and they don't want to give outsiders a chance. My first day, I ended up eating lunch by myself at a small table in the corner of the cafeteria. I didn't talk to anyone. This school was bigger than the last one I'd attended and the kids all looked meaner. I felt like I was in kindergarten all over again. The second day was just like the first. But on the third day, something unusual happened. As I was eating my lunch, this tall girl with wavy black hair came and sat with me. She introduced herself as Tina. We started to talk and she seemed nice enough, until she grabbed my purse and started to rifle through it. Once she'd found what she was looking for, my wallet, she pulled out my money, thanked me for my time and started to get up. I sat there frozen in shock for a moment. This girl had the audacity to talk to me for two minutes and then steal from me in front of the whole school! But

141

before I could do anything, I saw a petite blonde girl walk right up to Tina. The blonde girl grabbed Tina's hand, wrenched the money out of it, gave it back to me, and told Tina to stop being such a jerk. Tina, who was probably a foot taller than this girl, glared at her, then walked away. Teresa and I have been inseparable from that day forth. She stood up for me that day, and hasn't stopped taking care of me since.

The next day, I'm feeling much better about everything. Teresa and I ended up renting a movie and having a great night in. She made me see that I was overreacting and that I can't expect everything to be perfect all the time.

Right now, I'm on my way to work and I'm actually on time. I'm just congratulating myself, when my phone rings. One look at the caller ID tells me that it's my mom.

"Hello," I answer.

"One whole weekend went by without so much as a call," she says shrilly. "Your papa and I have been sick with the worry!"

"Mom, I told you and dad that I'd be spending the weekend at the beach with Teresa," I say slowly.

"Yes, but then did you lose your voice?" she asks accusingly.

"No," I answer, rolling my eyes.

"Then?" she says, as if that one word explains it all.

"Well, I guess I forgot," I answer honestly.

"You didn't even come to the *Mandir* yesterday because you were at your party sharty," she says. I will never understand why Indian parents insist on rhyming their words with words that aren't even real.

"It wasn't a party sharty," I say sarcastically. "I was at the beach."

"Well, whatever it was, you forgot about your parents," mom says finally.

"Listen, mom, I'm almost at work right now," I start. "How about if I come over for dinner later?"

It seems like I just said the magic word, because my mom's tone of voice changes completely. "Okay, I will see you this evening," she confirms.

I really do hate lying to my parents. But it was absolutely necessary to lie to them about my whereabouts this past weekend. So after they left my apartment, I called them from my phone while Shawn was filling up gas and told them that Teresa and I had decided to go to Wasaga beach for the weekend. This way I figured that I'd be covering my own butt. They trust Teresa, so I knew that there wouldn't be any issues. I know this all might sound strange. I mean, I'm 24, live on my own and still have to practically ask my parents for permission to do something. But that's the way it is in our culture. Honestly, I'm actually really lucky that my parents are so lenient with me. I remember this one girl I used to know when I was fourteen, Reena. She lied to her parents about everything, even if she wanted to come over to my house to watch a movie. She'd always tell them she was going to the library to study. Her parents once found out that she had actually been at the mall (with a boy!) instead of at the library, and they forbid her to leave the house ever again unless it was for school. I never saw much of her after that. I recently heard she was a stripper at some grimy nightclub. I think all those years of having such strict parents caught up to her and she decided to do something rebellious to get back at them. It's my theory that kids who have parents that refuse to trust them and always try to hold on so tight, are always the kids who turn out to be the most messed up. But who knows? Maybe Reena just needed some quick cash.

As I'm sitting at my desk, stuffing more papers into filing folders, I see Ravi approach me. What is it with this guy? I wish he'd just leave me alone. The two of us don't get along and there's nothing that can be done about it. Maybe I should tell him, so he'll give it a rest.

"Well I hope you're happy," he whispers, leaning over my desk.

"What are you talking about?" I ask him suspiciously.

"Roz broke up with me because she said she can't stand the sneaking around," he replies glaring at me.

"And you think that's my fault?" I ask him incredulously.

"Of course it is," he responds as if I've asked him something ridiculous.

"You've got to be kidding," I say rolling my eyes as I continue to file away. "I never threatened your relationship with her."

"Yes, you did," he insists. "You said that you would tell Tom about us."

"Are you insane?" I say my voice rising slightly. "I said that I could care less what you do with your personal lives as long as it's not on public display at the office. So, if you can keep your tongues in your own mouth, by all means you've got my blessing."

"Well, whatever," he continues. "All I know is that she got scared and broke up with me."

"Did you ever think to take responsibility for the break up?" I ask him, looking him in the eyes. "Maybe things just weren't meant to be, or you couldn't satisfy her or something."

He looks at me and frowns. "I can't believe you just said that."

"Well it's true," I tell him standing up. "Instead of blaming someone else, you should take a closer look at the relationship itself and figure out what went wrong. And when you do that Ravi you'll realize the truth, and I can promise you that it had nothing to do with me."

Ravi stands there for a second longer. He opens his mouth to say something, but I cut him off.

"If you'll excuse me, I, unlike some people around here, have a lot of work to do," I tell him in a falsely sweet tone.

"Fine," he says simply and turns to walk away.

I can't believe that I'm thinking this, but I actually miss my parents and having dinner with them. These are the thoughts that are floating through my mind as I'm on my way to their house, later that night.

When I was much younger, dinnertime was family time. My mom would cook some delicious Indian food, and we'd all crowd around the dining table for a wonderful supper. Dad would talk about work, mom would ask me how school had been and things just seemed so picturesque. Then as I got older, family dinners seemed to become more and more obsolete. Dad became busier with work, so did mom, and I became more occupied with my friends. I recently heard that having dinner on a daily basis with your family could actually reduce stress, which in turn can make you more successful in life. Maybe my family and I should eat together more often.

I walk into the house and call out for both of my parents. When neither of them answers right away, I shrug and go into the kitchen for a glass of water.

"There you are *beta*," I hear dad say from behind me.

"Dad!" I cry, giving him a hug. "I missed you."

"Yes, well your mother and I missed you too," he says, blushing slightly.

"It smells so good in here," I tell him. I notice the savoury spices from our dinner, wafting out from underneath the pots and pans that are sitting on the stove.

"Yes, your mother took a lot of time making the food," he says, nodding his head. "Uh, Janaki, there is something that I need to talk to you about before your mother comes down," dad says seriously. I rarely ever hear him use my full name. I'm all ears, knowing that this must be important.

"Okay," I say, prodding him on.

"Sit down," he gestures towards the table. "I know that you and your mother have your arguments here and there..." dad trails off.

I look at him questioningly. Where is he going with this? And why does he look so nervous? Oh no, please don't tell me that it's something bad. It's got to be something awful, or else he wouldn't be hesitating the way he is. I start to bite my nails, an old habit that I used to have when I was a teenager. Now the only time that I do it is when I know the worst is coming.

"Dad, you're scaring me," I tell him.

"No, no, don't worry. It is nothing big," he reassures me.

"What is it?" I ask, wishing he would just spit it out.

"Well, I think you are giving her the hard time," he says finally. "You should be easy with her. Ever since you are gone, she gets very upset after talking with you."

I feel a rush of guilt hit me. I always thought that my relationship with my mother hadn't really changed much since I moved out of the house, except for the fact that I don't get to talk to her or see her as often. But it never occurred to me that my words might actually hurt her. I just assumed that whenever we bickered it was just like we always had.

"I never thought of it," I tell dad honestly.

"Yes, well it is because you both are always the same," he says knowingly.

"What?" I ask. "I'm nothing like mom."

"You are more like her than you think," dad insists. "And you don't know how hard this change has been for her. Then she calls you and you take a bad tone with her."

I consider what dad's just told me. "You might be right," I say nodding my head. "I don't know why I do it, dad. I just automatically get so defensive when I talk to mom."

"Yes, that is why I thought I should mention it," he says.

At that moment, mom comes into the kitchen. She sees the two of us talking quietly and I can see her eyes narrow in suspicion. "What is going on?" she asks.

"Oh, nothing," I tell her. I can see she's not convinced so I change my tactic. "Mom, I missed you so much," I say, giving her a hug.

Mom stands still for a moment, in surprise. Then I feel her arms wrap around me. "I missed you too *beta*."

The fact that both of my parents are human as well always seems to slip my mind, as I'm sure it does for most kids. I normally see them as the parental unit. You know, they're there to take care of you, to keep you out of trouble, to discipline you, or to offer you advice. And then you automatically disregard anything they say because you assume that they don't know what they're talking about. After my recent wake up call, I'm starting to consider the thought that perhaps they do know what they're talking about. They are real people, with real problems of their own. They've probably been through a lot of what I'm going through right now, maybe just in a different way. And I know now that my mom's not out to ruin my life or anything. I need to be nicer to her. I vow to stop snapping at her like I always do...unless, of course she snaps at me first.

Okay, so I received my very first credit card bill today, and I think I'm having a panic attack. In the past I could shop 'till I dropped, and dad always took care of the bill. This time however, I have to remember to take deep, calm breaths and keep my cool. There's no way that I could've spent over $2000 this month on clothes and food alone. Of course the stuff that I bought was an absolute necessity. I mean, after ruining my clothes, I had to replace them, and food is something that no one can live without. Why on earth do people have credit cards in the first place? They're such a tease. You charge something and feel as if you're getting it for free. Then the creditors sit there and laugh as they send you the ridiculous bill at the end of the month. What a terrible concept. In fact, I think I should cut up my card right now so that I don't have to worry about it in the future.

Teresa, Julie and Christian are all on their way over to my place for some evening cocktails before we head out to some local bars and clubs. Shawn's away on business for the weekend, so I figured that it would be the perfect time for my friends and I to have a get together. Unfortunately, Christian's in a really sour mood. Earlier in the week, he walked in on Owen doing some very X-rated stuff with some random guy. Needless to say, Christian started screaming and yelling. He told Owen that their relationship was over and never to call him again. I believe a few dishes and vases were broken in the process.

"Hey guys," I say as I answer the door to find all three of them standing on the other side.

"Hey babe," says Julie, giving me a peck on the cheek.

Teresa gives me a quick smile before entering, while Christian looks indifferent.

"Ah, there are martinis waiting on the counter," I tell Christian specifically.

He looks as if I've just told him that the entire male population is now gay. "Thanks," he says, grinning. He practically runs to the counter and downs two martinis before looking back at the three of us. "Make sure that I don't get too trashed tonight," he tells us.

"Of course," says Teresa, sipping her own martini.

"Yeah, you know I want to have a good buzz and have a great time," he says, drinking his third martini in a more calm fashion. "But I don't want to get so drunk that I'm blubbering all over the place about how much I miss that cheating scumbag."

"We'll take good care of you," Julie coos.

Christian gives her a grateful smile. I tell the three of them to enjoy themselves, as I finish getting ready. I go into my bedroom, slip on my sexy navy skirt from Zara and match it with a glittery white H&M tank top. I scrunch up my hair, which I decided to wear wavy today and apply a last coat of mascara to make my eyes pop. After giving myself a quick once over and thinking that tonight, I could almost pass for Angelina Jolie, I head back to my living room and grab my own martini. I notice that we're running low. I guess Christian liked this Owen guy more than I thought, especially if he was able to polish off five martinis in the span of fifteen minutes. I finish my martini in one gulp, then start to make some more.

"So how's everything else going with everyone?" I ask my friends.

"Fantastic," says Christian with a scowl.

Teresa rolls her eyes, ignoring Christian.

Julie sits solemnly, without answering. This is unusual for her, since she normally can't keep her mouth shut.

"Okay, spill," I tell her, as I add an extra ounce of vodka to the shaker.

"There's nothing to spill," says Julie with a nervous laugh.

"Liar," I say narrowing my eyes.

"Fine," she says. "It's Vince."

"Oh no, what'd he do?" I ask with a hint of concern.

"Well, he's just so persistent," she starts, then pauses. "He offered to take me to France."

"What?" asks Teresa, her jaw dropping.

"Yeah, can you believe him?" says Julie, with a wave of her hand.

Something about the tone of her voice makes me suspicious. "You're not actually going to take him up on the offer, are you?" I ask.

Julie looks at all three of us, unsure of how to answer.

"Julie, no!" exclaims Teresa.

"Look, he really cares about me. And it's France! Do you know that I'll probably never have an opportunity like this again?" she says shrilly.

"Yeah, but come on, you're like using the guy," I say as I finish pouring out more martinis for us.

"I knew you guys would think like this," she says huffily.

"Yeah, because you know that he's only doing it to try to woo you," explains Teresa.

"Christian, what do you think?" Julie asks, noticing that he hasn't given his opinion yet.

"I say you take what you can from the bastard," he says, slurring his words slightly. "Guys are jerks, okay? And besides, he knows that he doesn't stand a chance with you. If he's still stupid enough to take you on an extravagant vacation, well then I say you do it. It's not like he doesn't have the money."

Julie looks at Christian gratefully. "See, he knows what he's talking about."

"You're going to take advice from the drunk guy who just got his heart broken?" asks Teresa, arching her eyebrow.

"You know what? I think I am," says Julie, almost daring us to argue.

I look at Teresa and know that there's no point in trying to convince her otherwise. That's the thing with Julie. Once she has her mind made up, Gucci would probably go out of business before she would change it.

We finish off our martinis then make our way out the door. Julie and Christian head out first, with Christian leaning heavily on Julie's arm. I grab my keys to lock up, when Teresa puts her hand on my arm. I can tell immediately that something's up.

"You guys go and wait at the car," I yell towards Julie and Christian.

"Okay," Julie waves her arm without turning around.

"So, what's going on?" I ask Teresa.

"It's about Luke," starts Teresa, biting her lower lip.

Anytime that I've tried to ask Teresa how things were going between her and Luke, she would automatically reply that they were fine, before changing the topic. Eventually, I had no choice but to give up and wait for her to come to me. What I do know for sure though, is that things between her and Gary are long over. She told the poor guy that she liked him more as a friend, and apparently he was so crushed that he went out and bought a whole new supply of socks.

"I knew it! I told you that he wasn't the guy for you, Teresa," I tell her, thinking about her and Luke.

"I had a feeling that he would do something to hurt you again. I should've paid more attention. Maybe if I'd harassed you about the situation everyday then you would've listened. Oh he's dead. Just wait until I get through with him. He's not going to recognize his face from his ass."

"No, Jackie," says Teresa, looking me in the eye. "You've got it all wrong."

"Well what then?" I ask.

"He's, well, he's ahh…" Teresa stumbles.

"Come on Teresa, you can tell me anything," I say soothingly.

"He's asked me to marry him!" she blurts out. "And I've decided to accept."

She waits a beat for my reaction. I'm at a complete loss for words. I don't know why, but I get a funny feeling with this guy. It's going to take much more than a marriage proposal for me to trust him. He's only been back in Teresa's life for like a month and he's asking her to spend the rest of her life with him? It just sounds so odd. But maybe I'm just being too pessimistic and I should give him the benefit of the doubt. I can see the expectant look on Teresa's face and decide to push all my thoughts aside. I know what she wants to hear, so I give it to her.

"Congratulations!" I exclaim, hugging her.

"Do you mean it?" she asks, still hugging me.

"Of course I do," I tell her, pulling back so she can see the happy smile on my face, a smile that I have to try my hardest to fake.

"Oh, you don't know what this means to me," she gushes. "I was so nervous about telling you. I thought that you would give me a long lecture and…well never mind."

"Me and lecture you? Never. And you know what?" I tell her, squeezing her hand. "You're engaged. Which means that tonight has to be extra special."

Teresa gives me a huge grin. "I'm so happy Jackie, honestly. Oh and on a side note, don't ever trash talk again. You could never beat up or threaten anyone if you tried. If I hadn't been so anxious, I probably would've burst out laughing at the thought."

I laugh with her and the two of us walk towards the elevator; one of us feeling very relieved and excited about the future, and the other trying to be happy for her.

I still cannot understand everyone's emphasis on marriage. I mean, sure, I want to get married at some point and time in my life. But probably after I've accomplished everything that I want to do, because let's face it, once you get married, that is where your priorities lie. You can't travel the world without taking your husband and kids along with you. You can't change jobs without worrying about whether you'll have to move, and if the money will still cover your expenses. You can't just pick up and go, you know? It's like being tied down for the rest of your life. You have to take into consideration not only your husband's well being, but also that of your kids. It just sounds like so much responsibility! By thinking this, I'm sure that I don't sound like the typical woman, who wants nothing but marriage and kids and who only enters relationships with those things in mind. I just think that guys might have the right idea. Why can't we just date and maybe even live together without having to make everything so concrete and final? I mean, what difference does it really make whether you have a piece of paper stating that the two of you officially belong to each other? To me, it just sounds like a way for the government to keep tabs on you. Or maybe I don't really care either way and I'm just slightly worried about the fact that Teresa's going to get married and leave me all alone.

Monday morning, I'm lying awake in my bed, willing myself to get up. I've got to be at work in exactly 45 minutes, which means that I'll probably be late as it is. I groan, then roll over, telling myself that I will sleep for exactly five more minutes.

It's not that I'm actually feeling tired today. I'm just feeling awful. I haven't spoken to Shawn all weekend, but that can't be it, because he's not supposed to be back from his business trip until tomorrow night. Maybe a small part of me was hoping he would at least call to tell me that he missed me. So that could be part of the problem. However, I know there's more.

Something has been nagging me ever since my conversation with Teresa this weekend. She went on and on about how Luke and her were planning on having a small and intimate wedding, and how they wanted to do it very soon, before the end of the month if they can manage. She wants me to be her maid of honour, of course. This lays a huge responsibility on me. I've got to help organize the whole wedding with her, because conveniently, Luke said that he's not good at that sort of stuff. So that just leaves Teresa, her parents, and me. I've also got to plan the stagette of the century, I mean this is my best friend getting married here.

All of these things should get me really excited, and instead, it all seems to depress me. It's not that I'm jealous, that much I can confirm. It's more the fact that my very best friend will be leaving me and entering a world that I may not know for a long time. She's going to be all grown up and married. She might as well move to a different universe.

I bury my head under the pillows as another wave of sadness hits me. Then I look at the clock again. I'm down to 30 minutes before I'm expected at the clinic. That's it, I decide. I'm calling in sick.

Half of me tries to argue and tell myself to suck it up, get dressed and go into work, with a happy smile on my face. But a bigger and more convincing part of me says that I really do feel sick, so it's not like I'd be lying. And besides, I'm sure that the folders will all be there tomorrow, waiting to be filed.

"Good morning, Roz speaking. How can I connect your call?" I hear Roz answer the phone.

"Hi Roz," I say, forcing myself to cough and play up the sick part. "It's Jackie. I'm not going to be able to make it into work today. I'm not feeling well."

"What a shame," Roz says sarcastically. "So you won't be able to ruin anyone's relationship today then."

This statement catches me slightly off guard. Ever since Roz and Ravi called it quits, I noticed that Roz takes every chance she can to ignore me. She even leaves the room when I enter it. I just assumed that it was because she was embarrassed since I caught the two of them practically shagging each other. But apparently, the real reason is that she hates me or something.

"Excuse me?" I ask her, wondering if maybe I hadn't heard her correctly.

"I said that it's a good thing you won't be coming in today, or else maybe you'll ruin someone else's relationship."

"What the hell are you talking about?" I say, remembering to keep up my sick voice.

"Look, you know what you did. Don't deny it," she says coldly. "We used to have the perfect relationship, until you came along."

"Okay, I don't know what your problem is, but just tell Tom that I'm sick," I say, beginning to lose my temper.

"Fine," says Roz, with a click of the phone.

I lay back in bed, pondering what that was all about, before coming to the conclusion that she must be jealous. She's trying to come up with some reason to hate me, and this is the best she can do. She's just like Ravi. The two of them have nothing better to do than blame other people for their own mistakes. I close my eyes, and fall back asleep without another thought.

I wake up around lunchtime, my stomach growling. I decide that I have no choice but to finally get up. Teresa's pending wedding and my conversation with Roz are temporarily pushed out of my mind, I get up, shower and dress. I decide that I'd better go out to get something to eat, since the thought of more cereal makes me want to hurl.

As I'm waiting in line at Wendy's, I feel a tap on my shoulder. I turn to see the one person who could make me feel even more miserable today.

"Ravi," I say slowly.

"Jackie," he responds. "I am on my lunch break, but I thought you were sick."

I look at him in alarm. Shoot, he's going to tell, and I'll be in so much trouble! They'll probably fire me. There goes everything. I'm already in debt, and without this job I'll probably just drown in it. Seriously, this is getting ridiculous. What are the chances that he happens to be at the same Wendy's as me? And why do I continue to bump into him so unexpectedly. He must be stalking me.

"Don't worry, your secret's safe with me," he says as if he can read my mind.

"Why?" I ask him suspiciously.

"Because, you never ratted me out when you had the chance," he says easily.

Oh, beautiful, wonderful karma. If I could kiss it, I would. I make a mental note to be nicer and do more good things.

"Well, I appreciate it," I tell him, before turning back to face the front of the line.

"Listen, do you mind eating with me?" he asks. "I hate sitting at one of those tables by myself. Plus I'm sure that you could use the company as well."

I roll my eyes. I luckily haven't really had to talk to Ravi ever since the time I told him to leave me alone. I don't know why he actually listened to me. But I knew that it was too good to be true, because here he is again, butting in.

"Actually, I'm getting it to go," I tell him.

"Well, I understand," he says. "But just think of it as you doing me a favour."

The thought of karma crosses my mind again and I dejectedly agree to eat with him, just because of the simple fact that if I don't, it'll come back to me times ten. I'll probably be forced to eat with him for like the next three weeks or something!

The two of us order, then head over to one of the plastic tables that have plastic chairs attached to them.

I don't wait for him to start eating, and instead, dig into my food. I'm half way through my burger before he says something.

"I wanted to apologize for blaming you about me and Roz," he says, sticking a fry in his mouth.

"It doesn't matter," I respond indifferently.

"Yeah, but it was still a stupid thing for me to do," he continues. "I was just upset about the way that things turned out, so I figured that I'd lash out at someone."

"Thanks for choosing me," I say half jokingly.

Ravi gives me a small smile. "Well, I don't know why, but I sort of like bugging you about stuff," he admits.

I look at him in amusement. Is he trying to flirt with me? I almost laugh out loud at the thought, and then push it out of my head, telling myself that I must be imagining things.

"Lucky me," I say sarcastically.

He shakes his head in response, and then changes the subject. "So how was your weekend?"

"It was good," I reply, not wanting to offer more information.

"Well, mine was a bust," he admits reluctantly. "I stayed home like an old geezer both nights."

My eyes widen in shock. The thought that anyone could stay home on a weekend never ceases to amaze me. I mean it's not like he's old.

"You're kidding," I ask. "Why on earth would you stay at home?"

"Well, I was supposed to go camping with a couple of buddies, but couldn't make it in the end," he says, taking a sip of his drink. "I had too much work to do for the clinic."

"Wow, now that's devotion," I say seriously.

"Not devotion, it's necessary," he replies matter-of-factly.

I nod, not knowing what else to say. There's an awkward silence, which Ravi breaks.

"You know, you're not as bad as I first thought," he says.

"Yeah, well you turned out to be worse," I joke.

Ravi smirks in amusement. Then the two of us go back to finishing off our meals and continue on with our easy conversation.

Wedding To Do List:
1. Call caterer (somewhere that serves Mexican food)
2. Call florist (a place that has blue roses for cheap)
3. Go dress shopping (finally something fun!)
4. Send out invitations (boring, boring, boring)
5. Plan stagette (stripper, liquor, what else do we need?)
6. Help Teresa find a hall (somewhere small and 'quaint')
7. Cake testing (why are wedding cakes always so dry and gross?)

This wedding planning is driving me crazy! Teresa said she wanted something small and private, but this is turning into something huge and extravagant. The guest list went from thirty people, to seventy and is now well over two hundred. I didn't even know she knew so many people! She's very specific about what sort of floral arrangement she wants, and she keeps on changing her mind about who should cater. First she wanted Mexican food, then she wanted Greek, and now she's leaning more towards Italian. I suggested that she make it a buffet, with a little bit of everything. She looked at me blankly as if I was talking gibberish. I wish Julie were here, so that she could take some of the load off of me, but she's enjoying herself in ritzy France. She calls on a daily basis to brag about how neither Teresa nor I knew what we were talking about and how she's having the time of her life. Christian on the other hand is so bitter and disgusted with the thought of marriage that he refuses to help. He claims that Teresa should be happy that he's even agreeing to come to the wedding.

To make matters worse, I've barely had a spare moment to go out with Shawn. Our schedules have been completely opposite. But I guess that this is what being in an adult relationship is all about. Who knows? All I do know is that if the wedding doesn't happen soon, I'm going to have a breakdown of some sort.

Later during the week, after I've recovered enough to go into work, I'm on my way over to Nalini's house. I haven't seen my little cousin in too long and the plan is to pick her up, and bring her back to my place. Then we're going to eat tons of junk food, while watching movies. I've already stopped by the video store and grabbed all the movies that Nalini requested. Unsurprisingly, they all have some sort of pre-pubescent teen girl starring in them.

"Hey Nalini," I call to her when I enter her house.

She rushes up to me and wraps her skinny arms tightly around me. "I missed you Jackie," she tells me.

"Aw, I missed you too sweetie," I respond. "So, you ready for a night of fun?"

"Yep," she nods, pushing a strand of hair behind her ear.

"Great," I say. I look up to find her parents approaching me.

"Hello Janaki," they both greet me.

"Hi Auntie. Hi Uncle," I respond pleasantly. "How're you?"

"Very good," nods Uncle gruffly. "So you are taking Nalini back to your house then?"

"Yes, that's what we decided," I say in agreement. I look at both of them awkwardly. I don't know why they're continuing to stare at me like that. "So, um, we'll just be going then," I say finally.

"Wait just a moment," says Uncle.

"Is everything okay?" I ask uneasily.

"Of course," says Auntie as if I've asked something absurd.

"We just wanted to tell you to be sure that you have Nalini home before nine," says Uncle.

I look from my Aunt to my Uncle, wondering what else is on their minds. Obviously it can't just be that they don't want me to keep Nalini out late. Auntie looks as if she's going to say something else, but then changes her mind.

"I'll have her home five minutes before nine," I promise them.

With that, I decide that I've had enough of the third degree. I grab Nalini's hand and usher her out the door, towards my car.

A few hours later, after we've watched the first movie, started the second, and eaten way too many sweets, I've pushed all thoughts of what's bothering Nalini's parents out of my mind. Instead, I'm just enjoying my time with the girl. She always manages to make me feel young again.

The two of us are laughing at something on the screen, the main character just tripped and fell into a garbage can, when Nalini pauses the movie and turns to me seriously.

"Jackie," she starts.

"What's up Nalini," I ask her, worry beginning to crease my eyes.

Oh no, don't tell me that it's something bad. She's going to tell me that her parents hate me and from now on will only let her hang out with Sonia. I knew it. This is just what I was expecting. I had a feeling that it'd only be a matter of time before people started to believe all the horrible things that Sonia says about me.

"Well, I like this boy in my class," she blurts out, her cheeks turning red.

I stare at her for a split second before bursting out laughing. "Is that all?"

"Yes, but what should I do?" she asks as if it's the end of the world.

"What's his name?" I ask before offering my 'big sister' advice.

"Devon," she replies shyly.

"Well he must be a cute one, if he's managed to catch your attention," I tease.

"Yeah, he is," Nalini says blushing again. "All of the girls in class like him."

"Well, I'm sure that he likes you the best," I wink.

"Mom and dad heard me telling one of my friends about him," Nalini admits. "They're angry with me."

"Is that why they were being so weird today?" I ask, everything clicking into place.

"Yes," Nalini nods her head.

"Oh good," I say relieved, before realising what I've just said. "I mean, I thought that they were pissed at me or something."

Nalini stares at me, her eyes wide. "Nope, just mad at me."

"Nalini," I start, seeing the worried look in her eyes. "It's okay. Listen, this is what you do. First, don't worry about your parents. They're just scared because their little girl is growing up and they know there's nothing they can do about it. So they might try to be a little bit overprotective. Second, talk to Devon. It's just that simple."

"Okay," Nalini says, thinking over what I've told her. "But how can I talk to him? He always has his friends with him."

"Well, you walk right up to him the first chance you get, and talk to him. You could ask him about homework or something," I offer.

"Yeah, you're right. I think I could do that," Nalini says.

"Of course you could," I encourage. "You're related to me after all. Talking to boys should be in your blood."

Nalini smiles and turns back to the movie. I can see that I've said the right words, even though I did have to tell a small white lie. The truth as we all know it, is that when it comes to talking to guys I really like, I end up making a complete fool of myself (hence the Shawn situation). Let's just hope that Nalini didn't get that gene in her blood.

The following morning, I'm sitting at my desk, congratulating myself. I can now finally see a dent in the stack of papers that need to be filed. I must be almost half way through. That means that within another month or so, I'll be all done and then I can move onto my next job. I haven't really given any thought as to what my next job at the clinic would be yet. I can just picture it now though. Tom is ecstatic because I've done the impossible, filed away every single paper that had been piling up at the clinic for years. He'll give me a raise and a week's vacation for all of my hard work. Then he'll tell me that when I come back, I'll be given my own office, complete with a secretary. Maybe they'll even train me to become a psychiatrist. I can just see Ravi's face now. He had to pay and go to school for years to become a doctor. And here I am, being offered the job without any of that hassle.

My cell phone rings, which brings me out of my wonderful fantasy. I answer it, and am about to tell off whoever had the audacity to disturb me, when I recognize Shawn's voice. Instead, I giggle in delight.

"Hey. How're you?" I say quietly. I'm not technically allowed to talk on my cell phone unless I'm off to lunch. If Tom walked in now, it might affect my chances of being promoted.

"I'm great," responds Shawn. "I was wondering if you wanted to get together for lunch."

"Sure. Where?" I ask.

"How about that deli place that's around the corner from your work?" he suggests.

"Sounds good," I agree. "I'll meet you there at noon."

We say good-bye, and then I quickly hang up the phone. I always get a little rush when I know I'm breaking the rules.

It's then that I see Ravi approaching my desk. The two of us have been making pleasant small talk with each other ever since our lunch on Monday.

"Hello Ravi," I greet him without glancing up from my files.

"Hey," he responds. "I just came by to ask you if you want me to pick you up anything for lunch."

I give him a weird look. We've been pleasant with each other, but we still haven't been exactly nice.

"I'm just asking everyone," he says, noticing my discomfort.

"Oh, ah, no thanks," I say hurriedly. "I'm meeting Shawn."

I don't know if I'm imagining things again, but I could almost swear that I see a trace of a scowl cross his face. But before I can be sure, it's gone.

"So you're going to see your pretend boyfriend again?" he asks, crossing his arms.

"He's not pretend you moron," I defend myself.

"Yeah, funny how you've been going on about him--," Ravi says when I cut him off.

"I have not been going on about him," I say heatedly.

"Well, we all still have yet to meet the guy," Ravi shrugs. "It's not like anything you've ever said before is the truth, so how can anyone believe you on this either?"

I glare at Ravi before answering. "I don't care whether or not people believe me. And anyway, why do you even care if I do in fact have a boyfriend or not?"

At that second, Roz enters. She takes one look from me to Ravi, then turns and walks abruptly from the room.

"Oh great," Ravi rolls his eyes. Then without another word, he takes off after her, telling her to hang on a second. This leaves me to continue my filing in peace. I force all thoughts of how much I wished I had a voodoo doll of that jerk Ravi out of my mind. And instead, I look forward to having lunch with my very real boyfriend.

That night, I'm just getting ready for bed, when I hear my doorbell ring. I groan and decide that whomever it is that is disturbing me at this hour better have a really good reason. I saunter over to answer it.

Then I stare at the person on the other side, baffled. "Sonia?" I ask, thinking that I must be dreaming.

She reaches over and pinches me. "Yes, it's me," she confirms as I yelp in pain.

"Ow," I say rubbing the spot where she pinched me. "What the hell do you want at this hour?"

"This hour? It's only ten-thirty," she responds haughtily.

Before I know it, she's pushed herself through my door, and into my home, uninvited. "Well, I do have to work in the morning you know."

"Yeah, you can wait five minutes," she says with a wave of her hand. "And believe me, I have no desire to be here any longer than that."

"Seriously what the hell do you want?" I growl at her now, feeling my anger rise.

"Well, I decided it was time to come over and look at the dump that you're living in," she smirks.

"Dump? Are you insane? Can you not see how beautiful this place is?" I ask in disbelief.

Sonia frowns. "I know. It's a shame that someone like you managed to get it. I was honestly expecting you to end up in someone's stinky, rodent infested basement."

"You're such a--," I stop myself before I go any further. Then I realise that she's in my home, insulting me, and there's no one there to stop me from saying what I please. "No, I'm going to say it. You're such a bitch," I spit at her.

Sonia continues to stand calmly in my living room, without saying anything. Her lack of emotion is just making me madder. "You've got exactly ten seconds to tell me what you want before I throw you out of here," I tell her, trying to calm myself.

"My parents forced me," she says simply. "I came by to drop off an invitation to my engagement. I begged them to not make me invite you, or to at least let me mail it out, but they insisted."

I can't believe my ears. Has the whole world suddenly decided to get hitched? Sonia roughly pushes the invitation into my hand.

"It'd be a great gift if you were unable to make it," she says rudely. Then she gives me a last glance, before heading out the door.

I stare at the invitation and the words 'Sonia weds Bobby' stare back at me. The engagement is for the first weekend next month. It states that the wedding isn't until after the New Year.

Yep, the whole world has gone insane. This all just confirms my beliefs.

I wake suddenly in the night to hear my phone ringing. My alarm clock states that it's exactly 3:02am. If this is Sonia interrupting me again, I swear she's going to regret it.

"Hello," I mutter gruffly into the phone.

"Jackie!" I hear Teresa's voice exclaim.

"Teresa?" I ask feeling totally out of it.

"Yeah, listen I've got some great news!" she bubbles excitedly.

"What's up?" I say, rubbing my tired eyes.

"Luke and I have decided to elope!" she practically screams into the receiver.

"You what?" I shout, jolting up in bed.

"Yeah, and listen, I still want you to be there. So Friday night, we've already booked a ticket for you to come with me, Luke and Nate, his best man, to Las Vegas," she finishes breathlessly.

"Teresa, isn't this all too sudden?" I ask, slightly panicked.

"Well, we talked about it and decided that we couldn't wait any longer to be together," explains Teresa.

"But I thought you wanted a big wedding," I press.

"I did, but then Luke made me realise that this way would be more fun and spontaneous," Teresa continues, completely unfazed.

"Okay," I say, at a loss for words.

"Great! So make sure you pack and stuff. We're going for the weekend. And remember, don't tell anyone!" Teresa warns.

"Of course I won't," I respond, feeling the sleepiness hit me again.

"Good night babe, and sorry for waking you," Teresa finishes.

"Good night," I mumble before switching off my phone.

I can feel my eyes burning, aching to be closed and continue sleeping. But my mind won't let me. I lay awake, worrying about Teresa and how I'm sure that she's making a huge mistake. I know Teresa, and I know that she's always wanted a huge fairy tale wedding. This must be all Luke's dumb idea. But then why would he want to rush the wedding date anyway, unless he really does want to marry her and be with her. I still get such a funny feeling about this guy. I can't quite put my finger on it. But maybe I'm just being the overprotective friend. I mean it is possible, however slim the chances, that he really has changed for the better. Maybe this time around he's here to stay and he'll treat her right. And then a sudden wave of guilt hits me. Here is my best friend, calling to tell me she's getting married tomorrow night, and all I can do is think the worst. I should be happy for her and be there to support her. I hit my pillow in frustration. My thoughts continue to twist and turn before I fall into a restless sleep.

Love. It's a simple four-letter word that is probably one of the most important ones in the English language. People say and do the craziest things when they're in love. Take Julie and Vince for example. Vince claims that he's in love with Julie and he's willing to spend an obscene amount of money in the hopes that maybe she'll feel the same way. Teresa and Luke on the other hand feel that they must let the world know that they're in love as soon as possible and have decided to put everything else on hold so they can run off to Las Vegas to get married. I once dated this guy who told me that he loved me and slept in his car, which was parked across the street from my house, for a week so he could prove it. Needless to say, I had to tell him that I'd get a restraining order against him if he didn't leave me alone. But what really is love? Is it when you care about someone so much that the thought of living without him or her seems impossible? Is it something that everyone interprets a little differently? Or is it just a word that people put too much emphasis on? Lately, I've been thinking the latter. I mean, sure, being in love would seem great. But then doesn't the feeling eventually fade? I've heard the fairy tale stories about two people falling in love, getting married and being together until the end, but how often does that really happen? It always seems that these people are friends of friends of friends whom you never meet, which makes the story sound like something someone made up to give themselves hope. My mom once told me that it's better for me to be with a guy who loves me more than I love him. But is it really better? Doesn't that seem unfair to the other person? And lastly, I can't seem to wonder how people can hurt the ones that they love. Cheating is the one issue that bothers me the most. A person will cheat on their significant other even if they're madly in love with them. It's things like this that make me feel like the concept of love is completely fabricated.

Friday at work passes by with me continuing to file away, ignoring Ravi's weak attempts to talk to me, and avoiding Roz's death glares. Before I know it, I'm packed, have been picked up and am on a plane with Teresa, Luke and Nate to Las Vegas. I can't believe that this is my second trip within the same week, making it my third time on a plane. You'd think that this would help me get used to the idea, but if anything, I seem to be getting worse.

I called Shawn before leaving my apartment, hoping that he might be able to offer a few words of comfort, and also to let him know that I was going to be away this weekend, but I was unable to get a hold of him. So I had to leave a message instead. I'm expecting him to return my call very soon.

But for the moment, it's taking every ounce of effort that I have to keep myself from freaking out. I'm clutching the arms of my seat so hard that my knuckles are white. Teresa's sitting on my right, but is too busy talking to Luke to notice. And I've got idiot Nate sitting on my other side.

My first impression of Nate when the three of them came to pick me up today was that he seemed really funny and cute in a nerdy sort of way. How wrong I was. Within ten minutes, I was praying that he would just shut up and sit quietly. Now, he still hasn't got the hint, even though I'm sitting right beside him, turning green in the face.

"So, then I said man, where do you think you are, a strip club?" exclaims Nate, laughing like a hyena.

I glance at him and give a forced smile, trying to keep from puking all over him. Though I don't usually get plane sick, for some reason, the combination of flying and listening to his anecdotes is making me feel nauseous.

"Dude, wait and the best part is, she freaked, threw her clothes back on and ran out of the house," he continues.

"Funny," I mutter shakily. He must be nuts. What guy in their right mind would turn down a woman who was standing half-naked in front of them?

"Yeah, and that's just the one story," he says completely unfazed. "You're going to flip dude, when you hear what happened the next day…"

Nate continues his story and I decide to tune him out. I catch Teresa's eye for help and she gives me an apologetic look.

After another hour of this, my ear feels like it's been talked off and I'm more nervous than ever. I tried to sleep, but it didn't help. I tried to tell Nate to read a book, and he unsurprisingly claimed that he hates to read. I keep on hearing the noise of the engine whir, and can't help from glancing out the window where all I can see is blue sky. I almost feel that at this point, jumping would be a more appealing option. The fact that I would even consider this tells me that I've reached my limits.

"So man, then, I couldn't believe it when he told me that he was a taxi driver! Yeah, the signs were all there and I should've been able to pick up on it. But seriously dude, I was like hello, where do you think are? That party was so not for taxi drivers. So then I turned to him and was like--" says Nate when I interrupt him.

"Listen," I bark. "I am not feeling well. I don't like to fly and with you babbling on beside me, it's making it worse. So will you please stop telling me your life story for like five minutes before I hurl all over you?"

Nate stares at me in shock. I can even feel Teresa and Luke's eyes on me. I almost feel bad for my outburst, before I hear it. Blessed silence. Not one of them has anything to say. I sit back, close my eyes and immediately feel calmer.

Las Vegas turns out to be a city like no other. We arrive at nearly midnight, but by the amount of lights that are shining throughout the city, and the people that are walking the streets, it almost feels as if it's late afternoon. The city is alive with loud music, people talking and laughing and cars driving by. Every shop, restaurant, casino, and club is open for business. I immediately feel my sleepiness leave me and am wide-awake, ready to have some fun.

After quickly checking into our hotel, Teresa and Luke decide not to waste another second and find a chapel that suits their taste. We decide to walk down the main strip, in hopes of finding one.

"Dude, you guys should totally get married in that one," points Nate enthusiastically. "It says you can dress up like Elvis and Priscilla."

I scrunch up my nose in disgust. While Nate did keep quiet on the plane after my tantrum, he turned back into his annoying self as soon as we arrived at our hotel.

"Teresa, you can't do that. It'd be so tacky," I tell her.

"No, I would never. I want us to get married as ourselves," she says, putting her arm around Luke.

We continue to walk and stare in awe. Teresa and Luke turn down countless chapels, saying that they're either too tacky, cheap or dirty looking. I consider telling them to just use this as a fun vacation and get married back at home, when Teresa's eyes widen in delight.

"That one!" she shrieks, pointing at a building not too far away.

My eyes follow the direction she's hurriedly walking towards and I can't help but nod in agreement. This is probably the most elegant chapel that we'll be able to find in Las Vegas. It's tall, white and upon entering, we can see crystal chandeliers hanging from the ceiling. I can't help but notice that the furniture does look a little bit ancient and the corner of the carpet is peeling, but I guess beggars can't be choosers.

"What do you think, sweetie?" Teresa asks, looking at Luke.

"Well, if you like it, then I have no objections," he says, giving her a quick smile.

We approach the front desk and behind the counter, a fairly attractive woman smiles kindly.

"A double wedding?" she asks, looking at Teresa and Luke, and me and Nate.

"Uh, definitely not," I reply, realising what she's implying. I'd rather eat my Prada purse than agree to marry Nate.

"Just me and Teresa today," Luke puts in.

"Too bad, we're having a sort of sale. The first couple is regular price and the second is half off," she informs us.

"Well, just us two today," Teresa says, seeing the disgusted look on my face.

"Alright then," she continues. "I just need you to fill out this paper work, pay the fee and you guys should be a happily married couple within the hour."

"Oh man, you're going to have a wife in an hour," Nate cries out, slapping Luke on the back.

"That's right," Luke says simply.

Is it just me, or does he look like I did on the plane right before I hurled? He seems nervous, almost as if he's having second thoughts. Before I can come to a conclusion though, Teresa and Luke are filling out the forms. The pieces of paper basically ask for their information and ask them to sign, stating that they are not under the influence of alcohol or any other drugs, and are agreeing to this union in a clear and conscience state of mind. Personally, I don't think that signing a piece of paper could prove that you are not drunk. And I never thought of Las Vegas as being one of the cities that wouldn't allow two people to get married if they were intoxicated. In fact, I'm pretty sure that most people who do get married in this city are drunk at the time. I guess that these are all just legalities though, so that you can't sue the chapel or something.

"Here you go," announces Teresa, handing the forms back to the woman.

"Great, now if you'll just have a seat, and we'll call you in just as soon as we're ready," she says with a smile.

The minutes tick by slowly. I can't help but fidget nervously. I never imagined that the day I'd be playing Teresa's bridesmaid, I'd be in Las Vegas, at some 24-hour chapel, wearing jeans and a t-shirt. I also never imagined that this is how Teresa envisioned her wedding. But it's too late for me to say anything to her now.

"And then there was this time that this crazy dude in a helmet came up to me and asked me if I was Jesus," says Nate, telling one of his stupid stories. "Of course I went along with it. You should have seen the dude's face! Man, he totally believed me."

"Nate, Teresa, can you excuse me and Jackie for a moment," Luke says suddenly.

I look at him in alarm. What the hell is this all about? Since when has Luke wanted to talk to me in private? I can vividly remember the last time we exchanged words privately; I told him that if he came within ten feet of Teresa again, I'd kill him.

"Sure. Ah, Jackie?" Teresa asks me, noticing my discomfort.

"It's fine," I reply calmly.

Luke stands up and I follow him down the hall. We both stand three feet apart for a few seconds too long.

"What's up?" I finally ask with a hint of suspicion. Then it dawns on me. "Look, if you want to bail and you think in your twisted mind that I'll be any part of it, you've got another thing coming buddy. Teresa is my best friend and if you even think for a second that I'll let you hurt her again, you'll be very sorry." I continue to glare at him, hoping that I look menacing.

Luke continues to look at me for a second before speaking. "This is exactly what I wanted to talk to you about."

"I knew it!" I seethe, my nostrils flaring. "How dare you! That's it. You're dead."

"No, no," Luke says, taking a step back. "I'm not bailing. I love Teresa very much. And that's exactly what I wanted to talk to you about."

"What?" I ask in surprise.

"I know the two of us have never exactly gotten along before," Luke persists. "But I want you to know that things are going to change from now on. I hope that this can be a new beginning for all of us."

I say nothing, at a loss for words. Out of everything I imagined, this is the last thing that I was expecting. I always assumed that once a jerk, always a jerk. I never thought that someone could actually change so much.

"Why should I believe a word that comes out of your mouth?" I ask, still a bit uncertain.

"Because, for the last few months, all I can think about is what an idiot I've been. I treated Teresa like trash, and I can't believe that she's actually willing to take me back. I know I don't deserve it, but I really do care for her. I can't live my life without her," he finishes.

Luke stands still, expectantly, and I look at his face. It's at that moment that I truly believe him because I can see it in his eyes. They're shining with the truth.

"Okay," I nod slowly, my own eyes unexpectedly welling up with tears of relief.

"You know, I just want the best for her."

"And I will try my best to give that to her," he confirms.

"You better, or else," I say, wiping away a single tear and giving Luke a small smile.

"Why didn't you tell me any of this before?"

"Honestly, I was too nervous. You scare me just a little," Luke admits and I can't help but laugh.

We both make our way back towards Teresa and Nate. Teresa looks from me to Luke quizzically.

"It's alright," I whisper to her and she nods in understanding.

"They've just announced our names," Teresa then tells us excitedly.

The four of us enter the hall and are slightly taken aback. The room is much bigger than I'd originally expected. A woman rushes towards us and tells Teresa that she must have something old, new, borrowed and blue. Teresa tells her that she is already wearing old, blue earrings. Then I offer her my DKNY necklace so she has something borrowed. And the woman gives Teresa a tiara, which is her something new. With all that sorted out, she tells Luke and Nate to stand at the front of the aisle, where the priest is waiting. She double checks that they have rings, then wishes us luck and exits the hall.

"She was a little too hyper for my liking," I whisper to Teresa, which causes her to go into a fit of giggles.

"I'm so scared," she reluctantly admits.

"The two of you will be fine," I assure her, and I mean it.

Then I hear the music start, which makes me think that these people do not waste any time, and the rest of the ceremony proceeds.

It really does turn out to be probably one of the nicest ceremonies that Las Vegas has to offer. Teresa and Luke deliver their impromptu vows without a flaw. Nate manages to keep his mouth shut. The music is beautiful and the priest is kind. We are even showered with flower petals as we all walk down the aisle at the end. Then we make our way out of the chapel and onto the vivacious streets of Las Vegas. I know that this is supposed to be a very happy occasion, however there's a very small part of me that can't help being just a little bit sad.

The weekend turned out to be a lot more entertaining than I'd originally thought it would be. Once Luke and I sorted out our differences, we were both much more easy going around each other. Teresa and Luke were both so excited to be married that they made sure to make the most of the whole weekend. Even Nate managed to back off a little, although I do remember one specific night when, after drinking too many beers, he proposed marriage to me. I obviously had to slap him out of it. Okay, so maybe I didn't actually have to slap him, but after having to put up with him the whole weekend I was just glad that I didn't break his nose or something.

I'm actually very content upon arriving at my apartment. I decide to shower and change into my pyjamas, and make it an early night since I have to be at work tomorrow morning. I'm just removing all of my make-up, when I hear a knock at the door. Getting a sense of déjà vu, I quickly dry my face and hurry to answer the door.

"Jackie, baby," says Mark, my landlord, sauntering into my apartment.

The last time that I saw Mark was when I was signing the lease paper. Luckily, at the time, Shawn was sitting right beside me, sort of like my bodyguard. Unfortunately, now he's nowhere to be seen. I'll have to deal with this loser on my own.

"Hi Mark," I start off pleasantly. I can't really piss him off, can I? "What're you doing here? I sent you the rent cheque already."

"Business, schmizness," he replies with a wave of his hand. Apparently, Indian parents aren't the only ones who rhyme their words; creepy guys do as well.

"Yeah, well I was just getting ready to tuck in, so is there anything you need?" I ask, hoping he'll get the hint.

"You can get me a drink," he says simply.

"I think you've had enough," I reply in disgust, noticing that he reeks of alcohol.

He laughs stupidly. "You can never have enough."

"Listen, this really isn't a good time," I insist, trying to be more blunt. "You have to go."

"This is my place honey. I'll go when I want," he says with a wink.

I stare at him horrified. Okay, I must be the stupid one. Why didn't I see this coming?

"It's like this," he continues. "I gave you a good deal on the rent. A damn good deal actually. And do you think I just did it out of the goodness of my heart?"

"Um, well I thought you did it because you and Shawn were friends," I answer lamely. At the time, it seemed logical. Now I could kick myself for being so naïve.

"Friends?" Mark spits out. "You can't be serious. I am a businessman. I don't have any friends. I make decisions based on what the outcome will be. And the outcome of this one is that you owe me. Big time."

It's then that I start to get the gist of the situation. "Okay, how about I pay you more for the rent then?" I ask hopefully.

"Baby, I've got plenty of money," he says, licking his lips. "What I want is you."

"Well, you can't have me," I reply icily. If this guy thinks that he can intimidate me, he's got another thing coming. After all of my years of clubbing, I've had plenty of experience dealing with disgusting jerks. The only small difference is that I've never been alone with one in my apartment. Apparently I've said the wrong thing, because I can see Mark's eyes narrow in anger.

"Okay, you need some time to think," he says, trying to keep calm. "I'm really not a bad guy. Just consider what I've offered you. You can even stay here for free, as long as you're willing to do what I ask, when I ask. It's a really good deal when you think about it."

I see him turning to leave, I close the door behind him, and I can't help but thank God. I promise myself to pray extra hard at the *Mandir* next week.

I can't believe the kind of stuff that women have to go through. It's so cruelly unjust. We have the obvious once a month pains, every month for like the rest of our lives. Then we have the whole pregnancy factor. I mean, who decided that it would be a woman who would have to carry that load for nine months, followed by more pain for who knows how many hours, until we squeeze another life out of us? And of course we have idiot men to deal with on top of everything. They'll act as if they really love us, and then cheat on us. They'll say that they will marry us, then bolt two hours before the ceremony. They'll even knock us up, and leave us without a second thought because they got scared. Then there's the whole equality of the sexes thing. Apparently, women are supposed to be treated as equals in the workplace. But count on a man to make a sexual pass at a woman and expect the woman to let it slide if she wants to keep her job, or in my situation, my apartment. There are also many cultures, like Indian for example, that still to this day think that when a girl is born, it is a sad occasion. Some parts of India will actually kill the baby girl as soon as it is born, which is something that makes my stomach turn. Also, in our culture particularly, girls have to put up with much more than boys when they're growing up. Even my parents would say things like, "*Beta*, you're a girl, so we have to be extra careful with you."

It took me years to come up with a logical explanation for this. Until one day, it occurred to me. What would they have to shield me from? Men. It's as simple as that. So after all this, it just seems like us women get the shit-end of the stick. But for some reason, whenever I think about how much easier it would be to be a man, I still would never give up being a woman. We can get whatever we want when we want, and we really do have more fun.

The next few days pass by in a blur. By the end of next week, I should be completely through with the filing at work. Ravi has been extra nice to me since his little accusation the other day. I've decided to play it his way for a while and have been pleasant with him as well. Roz still won't look at me, but I couldn't really care less about that fact. I've left three messages for Shawn, telling him to call me back as soon as possible. I need to tell him what his fantastic friend Mark tried to pull on me. Thankfully, Mark hasn't shown his face to me since. It's worrying me however, that Shawn has yet to call me back. Especially when I told him that it was something important. I'm all about casual, laid back relationships. But this is getting to be a bit too extreme for me even. Lately, I've been wishing that he would be around more often. It seems like I saw more of him when I first met him. Does he think that now that he has me, he doesn't have to make much of an effort anymore? If that's the case, he's got another thing coming.

I'm sitting on my couch in my apartment and painting my toenails one night when my phone rings. One look at the caller ID tells me that it's Shawn. Well, speak of the devil.

"Hello," I answer.

"Hey Jackie, I'm so very sorry," he starts apologetically. "Work has been crazy busy lately."

"Um, who is this?" I ask playing dumb.

"Come on Jackie. You know it's Shawn," he waits a beat. "Your boyfriend."

"Boyfriend?" I ask sarcastically. "Oh yes, I believe I was seeing someone once upon a time, long ago."

"Look, I'm going to make it up to you," he promises.

I hear my doorbell ring then. "I'm sorry, I'm a little busy right now," I tell him as I hang up the phone. That'll teach him a lesson.

I pull open the door and my jaw drops in surprise. "Shawn!" I cry out in shock.

He's standing right in front of me, cell phone still in hand and his other hand carrying a bouquet of the most beautiful flowers I've ever seen.

"I told you that I'm going to make it up to you," he says with a sly grin.

"You're still not forgiven," I tell him, taking the flowers and moving aside so he can come in.

"I thought so. Which is why I also brought this," he says picking up a box of chocolates from beside the doorway.

"Ferrero Rocher! They're my favourite." I exclaim, taking the box from him. "Well, this might be a good start. But you've still got a long way to go. So unless you've got a car hidden in that hallway, you can start explaining."

"Well," he starts, walking in and taking a seat on my couch. "Work has been so hectic. I got your messages, but not until today. I've barely had a spare moment to even eat or sleep! I can't believe it's been so many days since we've spoken. I'm sorry I didn't get back to you sooner."

I take a second to put the flowers in water and consider what he's just said. "Shawn, I really think that we could have something here, but it can't move forward if we don't see each other."

"What happened with Mark?" he asks. I notice that he's changed the topic and for the moment, I'm going to allow it.

"He's a sleazebag. He came here, drunk and made a pass at me," I say, summing it up for him.

"Are you okay?" he asks in concern.

"Yeah, nothing happened. But he basically told me that he expected it to if I wanted to continue living here," I explain.

"I'll fix it," Shawn promises.

"How?" I ask, raising an eyebrow.

"I'm going to have a talk with him. And remind him that if it weren't for me, his company would have lost millions," he says simply.

"You think that'll scare him enough to back off?" I ask, not totally convinced.

"Nope, but when I tell him that I can reverse what I did for him on a moment's notice..." Shawn trails off, grinning mischievously.

"I think that should do the trick," I say smiling.

"So how was Vegas? I wish I could've come," he continues.

"It was good," I reply easily. "Teresa and Luke are married. I'm willing to trust him now. She's happy. What more can I ask for?"

Shawn sits for a moment, nodding. I bring him a glass of juice, which he accepts.

"Look, I think we might need to talk," I say, bringing the conversation back to where it started.

"Okay," Shawn says, taking a sip of juice.

"How can this work if you disappear for days on end, like you just did?" I ask, jumping right into it.

"I said I was sorry," Shawn says with a shrug.

"Yeah and I accept that, but I mean, I haven't talked to you for like over a week, you know?" I say, a little uncertainly.

Maybe I'm making too big a deal of this. I mean we're just seeing each other exclusively. I've never been the type of girlfriend who needs to talk to her boyfriend ten times a day. But then again, how can we even consider getting more serious if we never get to talk to each other? Is once a day too much to ask for? All of a sudden I come to a shocking realisation. I do want to have a serious relationship, one that could possibly lead to marriage.

I sit on the couch, a little bit dazed. I didn't think until just now that I even wanted to get married, ever, and the thought scares me just a little bit. All this talk of weddings must be getting to my head. I try to think rationally.

"Look," Shawn interrupts my thoughts. "I like you Jackie, a lot. But my career is extremely important to me. I don't have time for anything serious. I need you to understand that."

I stare blankly at Shawn. "I do understand that."

"Great, so there's no problem," he says calmly. "Do you want to get something to eat?"

"Shawn," I start slowly. "I need a guy who's going to go the distance with me, and I'd like it to be you."

"Um, you're sort of freaking me out just a little bit," he says shakily.

"I know, I'm sort of freaking myself out as well," I say with a nervous laugh. "I like you too Shawn. But I want a guy who'll chose me over anything, and maybe that sounds crazy. Maybe that's impossible and too much like a fairy tale, but I can't keep wasting my time you know?"

"Oh, so you think you're wasting your time with me?" Shawn asks, hurt.

"No, no, I didn't mean it like that," I defend myself. "I just mean that I need to be in a relationship that is going to go somewhere."

"I see," Shawn says. He sits quietly for some time. I, for once, don't say anything because I'm too lost in my own thoughts. "I thought we were having a good time," Shawn says finally.

"We were," I look at the ground. "But it's just not enough anymore."

"I'm sorry you see it that way," he says. He stands up and walks towards the door. "But like I said, I don't have time for anything more serious than we have been. I'm not seeing anyone else, and neither are you. We care about each other. What more can you want?"

"More than that," I say quietly.

Shawn shakes his head. "I'm sorry, I can't. Goodbye Jackie. If anything changes, call me. And don't worry about the apartment. I'll still take care of it."

I stare at the closed door for a long time after Shawn leaves. I worry that I might've just let the best thing in my life slip away. I consider calling him and telling him that everything that I've just said is crazy talk and that of course I can deal with his busy work schedule. Then I realise that I deserve more than that. I shouldn't have to play second string to anything. I swore that when I moved out and was on my own I'd be more independent and that I'd go after what I wanted. Well, what I want is a man who'll put me above everything else. I put my head in my hands, wondering what the hell is going on with me.

Part 3:
All's Well That Ends Well

Text Messages:

Sender: Julie
Sent: 1:15pm
France was great! Ditchd vince frst chance I got. Partyyy 2nite at my place. Only tha most fab of tha fab invited. B here at 9. kisses!

Sender: Teresa
Sent: 1:39pm
Pik u up at 9 for juls party!

Sender: Christian
Sent: 3:03pm
Finally feeling well enough to get my groove on. Can't wait to have some fun tonite! See you there.

Sender: Teresa
Sent: 4:41pm
Havnt herd bak yet. Lemme know if u gonna b ready for 9.

Sender: Teresa
Sent: 6:37pm
Calld u. stil havnt heard from u. u ok?

Sender: Teresa
Sent: 8:02pm
Im comin over!

Depression. It seems to sneak up on you and hit you when you least expect it. Okay, so maybe I'm over exaggerating just a little bit. I guess I don't really have any reason to be depressed. I mean, it's not like I ruined thousands of dollars worth of clothing again. But this time, it still seems to hurt, though in a different way. I shouldn't be so upset with what happened. It's me who made the choice to end the relationship. You would think that knowing this would help comfort me. Unfortunately, this one time, being the dumper instead of the dumpee isn't helping the situation at all. If I wanted, I could call Shawn and go back to what we had. But I know now that I don't want that. And it's not because my best friend just got married, or because I feel I have to compete with Sonia or something else silly like that. I've seriously just come to realise that there's no point in having a relationship with someone if it's not going to go anywhere. I could spend my whole life going from random guy to random guy and by the time I reached forty or fifty, I'd end up alone. Instead, I know that I want someone with whom I can build a future. And while this thought might still scare me, it also gives me just a little bit of hope and excitement. It gives me something to look forward to.

For yet another time, I hear a knock on my door. I bury myself under my covers, which is where I've come to spend the majority of my time, and pray that whomever it is leaves.

"I know you're in there!" I hear Teresa's shrill voice yell.

"Go away," I yell back. "Please, just leave me alone!"

"Not until you talk to me," Teresa insists.

"I have nothing to say," I yell dramatically.

"I will break down the door, you know," she informs me defiantly.

"Try it," I say, turning over in my bed.

All of a sudden, I hear a loud thump hit my door. "Ouch!" I hear Teresa scream in pain.

I bolt out of bed and hurry to open the door. "I didn't actually expect you to do it!" I tell her exasperatedly. I look at Teresa, who is standing triumphantly with a smile on her face.

"Well, I didn't, so don't worry," she claims.

"What?" I ask in slight confusion.

"I knew that'd get you to open the door," she pushes past me and enters my apartment.

"What hit the door then?" I persist in bewilderment.

"My bag," she says simply. "You know, they're good for a lot more than carrying junk."

I look at her, see that she is in perfect condition, and decide to go back to sulking. "I'm going back to bed."

"No, you're not," she insists. "You're getting ready so we can go to Julie's party."

"Thanks, but no thanks," I say retreating to my room.

Teresa completely ignores me, walks towards my closet and pulls out an outfit for me to change into. "I think you'll look fabulous in this."

"Teresa, please, I really don't feel like it," I moan.

"Why? What's wrong?" she asks.

"I broke up with Shawn," I mumble.

"You what?" she cries out. "But Jackie, why?"

"Well, at the time I knew, but now I can't seem to figure it out," I say, pulling the covers up tighter around me.

"What're you talking about?" Teresa asks, worriedly.

"It wasn't going anywhere, Teresa," I try to explain.

Teresa puts down the D&G skirt she wanted me to wear and instead, comes and sits on my bed. "But it's not really like you to care about stuff like that. Do you want to talk?"

"I know it's not like me," I grumble. "I don't know what happened. I mean we haven't even been dating for a super long time. But I hadn't talked to him in so long, and I guess that made me realise that I wanted more. Then he came over to apologize and before I knew it, I had told him that since this relationship had no future, I didn't want to continue it."

Teresa says nothing, and instead wraps her arms around me. I can feel myself starting to feel better. It all doesn't sound nearly as bad when voiced out loud.

"Does it sound lame?" I ask, still a bit unsure.

"No, it doesn't," she confirms. "It just means that you're growing up."

Much later, I've tried to drown my sorrows in alcohol as usual at Julie's party. Unfortunately, before I was able to get successfully intoxicated, I started to feel sick. So after about three drinks I had no choice but to lay off the liquor, or spend the rest of the night in the washroom, with my head over a toilet. I chose the first option.

Julie definitely knows how to throw a crazy party. I'm standing in the corner of her condo, surveying the scene. Teresa and Luke have gone to get more drinks from the bar, Julie is playing the perfect hostess, and Christian has yet to show his face. As I stand by myself, I realise once again, how many eclectic people Julie really knows. This girl will befriend any and everyone! There's the group of sophisticated men standing on the other side of the room, wearing suits. There are the 30-year-old men who act like they're still stuck in high school, sitting on the couch and chugging beer while giving each other high fives. There's a group of wannabe models that are standing snootily, and making sure not to touch anything. There are also the few nerdy Bill

Gates type men, wandering the place, trying to see if tonight will be their lucky night.

I'm sipping my non-alcoholic margarita, when someone who I haven't noticed yet wanders up to me.

"So, who invited you?" asks Mr. Goth King with an edge in his voice.

Now I know I've seen everything. Where on earth did Julie meet this guy? He's wearing all black and more makeup than me, including black lipstick, eye shadow, eyeliner, and even nail polish. On a side note, I wonder where he gets his nails done because they look fab.

"I don't really see how that's any of your business," I reply stiffly.

"Whatever," he mumbles. "You got a light?"

"No, I do not," I say in my most 'leave me alone' type voice. There really is no reason for me to be so rude to him. I'm not prejudiced or anything. It's just that I really don't feel like talking to anyone at the moment.

"What's your problem?" he asks.

"Look, I don't have a problem okay? I'm sorry I don't have a light so you can light up your joint," I say, annoyed.

"I don't smoke weed," he tells me, now looking annoyed as well.

I immediately feel bad and begin to apologize.

"Bitter bitch," he says, before I can get the words out. Then he turns to walk away, leaving me alone once again.

I don't have any time to ponder upon what just happened because I feel someone come up behind me.

"Sounds like he's the one with the problem," says a familiar voice.

I turn around to find someone who makes me realise that now I really have seen everyone at this party.

"Ravi, what're you doing here," I ask. I'm not even surprised to see him. Apparently, we're destined to bump into each other randomly like this.

"I came with my friend, I think you just met him," he jokes.

I can't help but let out a small laugh. "Right, like that guy's your friend?"

"Okay, you caught me," he says putting up his hands. "But I did come with a friend. He's abandoned me though, so I guess I'm stuck with you for company."

"You say that like it's a bad thing," I comment. "What's your friends name anyway?"

"Cedric," he replies. "Oh look, here he comes now."

I look up to see Julie approaching us with some guy on her arm. He's actually very handsome. I can tell that Julie's found her flavour of the night. Poor Vince didn't even get an invite to the party for this exact reason. Julie wouldn't have been able to fool around with anyone else if he had been there.

"Hey Jackie," says Julie with a slight slur, which tells me she's had one too many drinks. "You remember Ced, the super sexy bartender from Devil's?"

My mind quickly flies back a few weeks in time and I vaguely remember Julie flirting with some bartender. Now that I look closely at him, he does look familiar, and still looks very much like Paul Walker.

"Of course," I reply politely. "How're you."

"I'm awesome, and you?" asks Cedric, making him sound like a surfer.

"Well, you two talk for a minute, I've got to sneak Jackie away. Be right back," says Julie with a wink.

She grabs my arm and pulls me into a corner. "Teresa just told me you were upset because of this whole Shawn situation, and now you're off playing the field already?" she pauses for dramatic effect. "I can see I've taught you well!"

"Julie, I'm not playing the field," I try to convince her.

"Well, from what I saw, he's cute and Ced told me he's single," she replies with a sly smile.

"I know that. I know him. I work with him," I explain.

"Well, if my co-workers looked like that, I'd never leave the job," she says grinning.

"Look, his name's Ravi, and there's nothing going on between us," I continue to persist.

"Ravi?" she asks quizzically. "Not the same Ravi that your parents tried to hook you up with, who you found out you also work with?"

"Yes, the one and only," I respond, seeing that she's finally getting it.

"Well, this arranged marriage thing doesn't sound so bad," she says mischievously. "Especially if there are guys like him out there."

I can't help but laugh out loud. "You're nuts."

"Well, whatever. Just thought I'd give you my advice, which in case you can't tell, is to go for it!" she says finally.

"You'd tell me to go for it if he was a tight rope walking clown who travelled with the circus," I joke.

"Yeah, well a man's a man," she says with a shrug. "And now if you'll excuse me, I've got to get back to Ced."

"Sure, you go," I reply, giving her a little push. "Great party by the way."

"Thanks, ta ta. Enjoy yourself," she calls with a wave.

I see her saunter back towards Ced, whisper something in his ear and pull him away from Ravi. I can see Ravi glancing at me for help, so I decide to give him a break and let him enjoy a few more minutes of my company. Who knows, maybe Julie's onto something?

If there's ever been a night that I wish I could go back in time and redo, it would be last night. I ended up talking to Ravi throughout the rest of Julie's party and one thing led to another, and let's just say that we did a little more than talk. Today, I woke up and totally regretted it. But when I reached for the phone to tell him that I'd made a big mistake, I saw that he'd already called to leave me a message, and tell me how much fun he'd had the night before. Damn Julie. This is all her fault for putting crazy thoughts in my head. There's only one thing that I can do now. And that is to avoid him at all times. This is going to be tricky, as we work together. But I know it can be done. It has to be done, because I'm too embarrassed and scared to talk to him otherwise.

So, on Monday morning, I put on my very best 'plain Jane' outfit, pull my hair back into a tight knot and decide to play the part of the silent employee. I will not talk to anyone, and hopefully my outfit will help me be invisible since it is very bland.

As I enter the office, I don't see Roz giving me the cold shoulder like she always does. Instead, I see Tom sitting in her place. Perhaps she's been fired? I'd feel terrible if this were the case, although I realise guiltily that a small part of me would feel a little bit relieved. She's been making the office atmosphere so awkward! Maybe after I get promoted, I'll be able to put her in a more suitable position elsewhere.

"Hi Tom," I say with a wave. "Where's Roz?"

"Roz has called in sick," he replies. "I need you to manage the phones and greet the clients today. Do you think you're up to it?"

"What about the files?" I blurt out as if it's the end of the world.

Tom laughs and I blush, deciding to go along with the fact that he thought I was joking. "They can wait until tomorrow. You know they won't disappear or anything," he replies, still smiling.

"Yes, of course," I reply, all business like again. "You can count on me."

"I know I can," he confirms. "So, all you have to do is answer the phone when it rings, and all of the extensions are listed here. And check the clients in when they come for their appointments. The appointment book is here," he tells me hurriedly.

I nod in understanding and before I can ask any questions, he's gone. I take a look at the desk, drop my purse onto it and settle myself into Roz's chair.

I'm just reapplying my lipstick, thinking how easy this is going to be and that this is the first step in my promotion, when the phone rings.

"Hello?" I answer.

"Yes, hello," responds a high-pitched voice. "I'm calling to confirm my appointment for today at three?"

"And your name is?" I ask.

"Cynthia," she replies.

It takes me longer that I'd hoped to find her name written in the three o'clock spot. This is because I have to check every single appointment book, since every doctor has his own. I suppose that I could've just easily asked her what doctor she was coming in to see, but the thought of hearing her super squeaky voice for longer than necessary, makes me shudder.

While I've got Cynthia on hold, the next line starts to flash.

"Hello?" I answer once again.

"Hello? You can't answer the phone by saying hello!" nags an all too familiar voice.

"Very funny, Roz. But you're not here to tell me what to do," I shoot back.

"I called to make sure that you hadn't already made a mess of everything," she takes a pause to cough violently into the receiver. "When you answer the phone, say 'Hello, you've reached the Burns clinic. How may I help you?' Then you have to wait and see what they say."

"Hello, you've reached the Burns clinic. How may I help you," I reply back sarcastically.

"Much better," says Roz. Apparently sarcasm isn't one of her skills. "And that's all I need thank you very much."

"Bye Roz," I say, annoyed.

I sit and think about how weird she is for a moment, before I realise that I was supposed to be confirming an appointment. I look back through the books, locate the appointment in question, and then click onto the line to tell Cynthia that we will see her today at three. Unfortunately, she's gotten tired of waiting and has hung up.

The next hour passes by in the same sort of fashion. I answer the phone calls, and only manage to screw up two more times. One man is a telemarketer and calls to sell glass bowls. I happen to get so caught up in a conversation with him about how a glass bowl is made, that I hang up on a client who wanted to schedule an appointment.

Then, another client calls, this time a male with a deep booming voice, and he tells me that he's all better and doesn't need to see Richard, the psychiatrist, anymore. I don't know what to do, because upon looking at the appointment book, I can see that he's scheduled every other day for the next two weeks. Well surely Richard wouldn't have scheduled the man's appointments if he didn't think it was necessary. I'm just about to tell him that I'll have to let Richard know, when all of a sudden, the man starts to yell at me, telling me that his house is on fire. I immediately call 911 and tell them to send a fire truck over. In all of the hustle,

Richard actually sweeps by the front desk, notices my panic and asks me what the problem is. Upon hearing about the man whose house is on fire, he stands still for a moment before breaking into a kind smile. I think that he must be cracking under the pressure. Richard then lays a hand on my shoulder and tells me that the man who called is a patient who is known to call every now and then and invent new situations about how he is going to die. Roz knows about him (funny she didn't mention), and we are to transfer his calls straight to Richard's voicemail.

I smooth back my hair, which must look a mess, and feel slightly calmer. It's then that Ravi enters the office. One glance at the clock tells me that it's almost ten thirty. Well he's had a bit of a lie in today, I think. I've had a chance to glance at his appointments and know that he's only got two throughout the day. Lucky him, he can lie back in his office, maybe take a nap, and then head out of here early.

"Hey Jackie," he says casually, approaching my desk.

I follow the plan and ignore him completely. Instead I picture myself lying on a beach in some Caribbean island.

"I said hi," Ravi persists.

I twiddle my fingers and when he sees that I'm not planning to answer, he leans closer to me. Man, this guy can't take a hint!

"Okay, I get it," he whispers. "But I did want to tell you once again that I had a good time the other night. Have a nice day."

With that, he walks towards his office and I'm left alone, all thoughts of the beach out of my mind. A very small part of me tells me that I'm being very immature about the situation. But another, more convincing part tells me that Ravi probably just wants to get more action, so he's only pretending to be nice. I don't know how he can be so cheap, or on the other hand, think that I'm so cheap. But this thought does put the whole 'ignore Ravi' plan into better perspective, making me decide to follow it through until everything becomes less awkward.

Later on, I've managed to make it through the day playing receptionist. After much persuasion, Tom was able to convince me that my minor mistakes were not going to get me fired. I actually told off one of the clients because I thought she was yelling at me, but it turned out that she is just a loud talker. Cynthia, the woman who I had left hanging, showed up promptly at three and complained to Tom about my lack of professionalism over the phone. Tom managed to calm her down and whispered to me that Cynthia was known to complain a lot. But other than those two incidences, the day passed by smoothly.

I'm walking towards my car when I hear footsteps, running to catch up to me.

"Jackie, wait," calls Ravi.

I continue walking and ignore him, picturing myself on the beach once again. As I'm fumbling for my keys nonchalantly, he reaches me and puts a hand on my arm to stop me.

"Why are you ignoring me?" he asks breathlessly.

I decide to whistle to try and block out his voice.

"I'm not letting you go like this," Ravi says, rather sternly.

I finally see that I have no choice. Damn, and I was almost feeling the warmth of the Caribbean sun. I turn and look at him. "This better be good, you know I could almost smell the salty ocean air."

He looks at me like I'm talking nonsense. Apparently he doesn't have much imagination.

"I just want to know why you're acting like a stranger," he admits.

"Because, I know what you're after," I reply simply.

"And what would that be?" he asks, raising his eyebrows.

"It's okay, you're a guy Ravi. It's only normal for you to think this way. But I just don't want things to get weird with us at work, so I thought that it'd be easier if we just forget that anything happened," I say opening my car door.

Ravi thinks for a moment, then realisation dawns on his face. "Jackie, you're wrong. You think that I'm only trying to talk to you to get in your pants? That's insane! I know you're not like that."

I shrug, but say nothing. He's obviously lying. I've heard it all before.

"Look, you think you know what I'm all about, but you have no idea," he insists.

"Ravi, I told you, it's okay. What happens between us doesn't really matter to me," I say, knowing that as soon as the words are out of my mouth, I'm the one who's lying. It does matter to me. I step back, starting to get confused.

"Do you know why I broke up with Roz?" Ravi asks quietly.

"You broke up with her? I thought she broke up with you," I respond, feeling butterflies in my stomach.

Ravi shakes his head. "It's because I couldn't seem to get you out of my head. You were wrong Jackie. You had everything to do with my break-up with Roz. I really like you," he blurts out. "I've always liked you."

It's as if those words are magical, because everything seems to whoosh into place. I see the first time that I met Ravi at my house, and all of our meetings afterwards in sequence. I see us being annoyed with and rude to each other at first, then teasing each other, and then finally the night at Julie's party. I know that that night at her party is probably the most fun I've had in a long time.

"I've got to go," I say, feeling that I need to get away to sort out my thoughts. This is just too much to take in at the moment.

Ravi nods in understanding and I'm grateful that he doesn't reach out and try to kiss me passionately, or do something else cheesy like they do in those romance novels.

"I'll call you," I tell him, getting into my car. I know then that I'm speaking the truth. I glance back once in my rear view mirror at Ravi, and I can't help but wonder what I've gotten myself into.

A moment of clarity can be defined as a turning point in your life when everything seems to fit into place and make sense. Now, I'm not so deluded as to think that when Ravi admitted his feelings for me, I felt that I was having that sort of moment. However, I do think it came pretty close. That moment, everything that had happened between Ravi and me seemed to make sense. No wonder there was always some sort of tension between us. It's like when you're in grade school and a boy teases you or pulls your pigtails because he likes you. Only, fast-forward twenty years and apply that sort of attitude in the office. The more I seem to think about it, the more I feel like maybe, just maybe deep down inside I've felt the same way as well, which is partially why I ended things with Shawn the way that I did. I know it sounds crazy. I know this sort of stuff doesn't happen in real life. But I also know that there's got to be a bigger reason as to why we continuously found ourselves at the same places at the same times. Maybe the concept of fate isn't as farfetched as I once thought it was. Maybe this is the way that fate really works. It makes the absurd seem normal and possible.

Pros:
1. he likes me
2. he's smart and educated
3. he's Hindu
4. my parents know him and his family

5. he's cute
6. he's a good kisser

Cons:
1. I just came out of a relationship
2. how do I know he's not lying about everything
3. we work at the same place…apparently against the rules

Okay, so I know that it might be unethical and maybe even a little mean to write a list of good things versus bad things about a person. I mean, on Friends, when Ross did it to Rachel and she found out, she flipped and it almost destroyed their relationship before it even began. I'll just make sure that I burn the list before Ravi has a chance to come across it. Anyway, I had to make the list because I find that weighing out the pro's and con's can help to sort things out. It's a nice little trick that I've picked up from Nalini.

I've spent all evening trying to figure out where to go from here. Taking a look at my list, it seems obvious that since there are more pro's, I should just tell Ravi that I want to give us a shot. But a little voice is still making me unsure. I don't want to get into anything that isn't going to go anywhere. I just came out of a dead end relationship. I almost feel like a yo-yo, just bouncing back and forth between my jumbled up thoughts. I know exactly what will help to untangle them.

Teresa and I meet at Tim Horton's, which is exactly half way between our homes. We order our teas, and then find a private spot in the corner to talk.

"So what's the scoop? Julie mentioned to me that you wandered away with Ravi the night of the party," Teresa states. She knows me well enough to know that that's exactly what I wanted to talk to her about, without me even having to utter a word.

"Yeah, and well I guess I might've gotten a little carried away," I tell her. Then I continue to tell her in great detail the rest of the story, ending with the fact that Ravi's now practically in love with me.

"He's what?" Teresa shrieks, spilling a few drops of her tea.

"Okay, so maybe love is a bit of an exaggeration," I say, wiping up the tea. "It's actually more of the 'like' stage right now."

"Oh, don't do that," exclaims Teresa. "I was about to have a heart attack and tell you that maybe the doctor now needs a therapist of his own. How tacky would that be anyway, eh? It's like one of those sappy movies if he had told you that he was in love with you."

I cut Teresa off before she can ramble on anymore. "So you see my predicament then? I'm so confused that I just feel like getting away from it all."

"Okay, what's bothering you about it? You've got a guy who's totally into you. Wow, it almost sounds as bad as those poor kids who're starving in Africa," Teresa jokes.

"No sarcasm, please," I frown. "How can I get into something again so soon?"

"Back up. Who's asking you to get into something so hot and heavy right away? He likes you, and by the sound of it, you like him. Date him. Then decide if you want to take the next step," Teresa says simply.

"I just don't know," I bite my lip. "With Shawn it seemed easier. I mean, he was so confident, and sexy. Ravi's more down-to-earth and… I don't know. Like the kind of guy my mom would like. And I actually know my mom would like him, since she tried to fix me up with him in the first place."

"Are you listening to yourself?" asks Teresa, throwing up her hands.

"I know. I'm nuts," I nod.

"Totally bonkers," she agrees. "Do you remember what you told me when I was talking about Gary and Luke?"

"Nope," I shake my head, not even bothering to think.

"It seems like the main thing that's holding you back is like the image or something. Well, you said something to me before that really made sense. I believe it went something like 'if that's the only thing holding you back then you should totally go for it'," says Teresa with a smile.

"I said that?" I ask quizzically. "Doesn't really sound like something I would say."

"Yeah, who knew that you would actually say something that was smart," Teresa smirks jokingly.

"Oh stop," I say, slapping her hand lightly. "So you think that I should give him a real chance?"

"Definitely," she replies.

I think for a moment about what she's advising, and realise that it's exactly what I wanted to hear. Deep down, I know that talking to Teresa was just an excuse. I've liked Ravi for a while now, even though I pretended that I didn't. I do want this to go somewhere, and I even get the feeling that it will.

"Wait, what happened with you and Luke?" I ask, suddenly remembering the fact that they're married.

"What do you mean?" she asks innocently.

"Uh, you guys got married! I meant to ask you days ago, but I guess I got carried away with my own issues." I explain.

"It's okay, I figured. And besides, there's nothing to tell, or trust me, I would've blurted it out by now," she answers.

"Did you tell your parents yet?" I ask.

Teresa giggles. "Nope, not yet."

"What?" I shriek. "You're still going along with the wedding plans as if you aren't already married? When do you plan on filling them in?"

"Well, I thought that I'd do it when I could shock them the most," she says with a glint in her eye. "You know, one night when we're having dinner, and dad's going on about work. Then I'll just pop out and say, 'Oh, by the way, Luke and I already got married so you don't have to bother with the wedding details anymore.'" Teresa finishes.

"But why?" I ask, slightly confused.

"Well, it's going to shock them anyway," she starts. "I figure that I might as well get the most shock value possible."

I look at Teresa, and shake my head taken aback. It's not really like her to try and create the most drama possible. It's almost as if she's taken a page out of Julie's book.

Later as I'm entering my apartment building, I'm tired, exhausted and ready to sleep, even though it is still very early. I can't wait to take my Nine West shoes off and stumble into bed. I'm just stepping off the elevator and am walking towards my door when my jaw drops in shock. Sitting cross-legged in front of my door is a man. And not just any man, but the very man who's had my head filled with all of these jumbled thoughts.

"Ravi, what're you doing here?" I ask surprised.

He looks up at me in relief. "I guess I'm bumping into you on purpose this time," he replies, standing up.

"Um, you ever heard of calling?" I ask sarcastically.

"I would've, but I figured this way was better," he says without missing a beat. "Plus, I figured that it would be worth it, just to see the look on your face. Your friend Julie gave me your address," he continues to explain.

I make a note to call Julie and have a word with her about giving out my personal details to strangers. Then again, I guess that Ravi wouldn't exactly qualify as a stranger anymore. Scratch that. I'll just call her and have a word with her about giving out my personal details without warning me first.

"Alright, come inside," I say finally. "Do you want something to drink?"

I rummage around the kitchen for a glass of water for myself and hear Ravi decline my drink offer.

"So…" I trail off, finally coming and sitting beside him on my couch. I place my glass of water slowly on the table and then glance at him, beginning to feel those damn butterflies in my stomach once again.

"Look, I meant to give you time," he starts hurriedly. "I mean I know that what I've sprung on you probably came out of the blue."

"Well, not exactly," I interrupt him. I can tell that the poor guy's probably more nervous than I am. "At first it did, but then it started to sound, I don't know, ah, nice," I finish lamely.

"Nice?" Ravi asks, confused.

"Yeah, well at first I was like whoa, then I was like okay, but then I was like I just broke up with someone and so did you, and then it seemed impossible, but then I thought who knows, you know?" I ramble on.

"Um, no," Ravi frowns. "You'd have to be mental to understand that."

"Sorry, sometimes I don't make sense when I'm anxious," I admit, taking a deep breath.

"That's sort of cute," Ravi smiles.

We both look at each other for a moment, neither of us daring to talk quite yet. I finally decide to break the silence and just say what's in my heart.

"I'd like to give this a chance," I blurt out.

"Let's give us a shot," Ravi says at the exact same time.

"What?" We both cry out slightly flustered.

"Wait," says Ravi, putting up his hands. "You go."

"Okay, well, at first I was like," I start.

"No, please, not that again," Ravi pleads.

I can't help but laugh. "Okay, I do like you," I say simply.

"Good," Ravi smiles finally. "Man, you know how to tie a guys stomach in knots."

"Yeah, I do have a way of doing that," I grin.

"So, how about I pick you up tomorrow night?" he asks.

"Where are we going to go?" I ask curiously.

"It's a surprise," he responds mysteriously.

"But what am I supposed to wear?" I ask now slightly worried.

"What you're wearing now would be fine," Ravi responds, laughing.

I look down at my jeans and T-shirt and frown. "I can't wear this again tomorrow!"

"Listen, don't worry about what to wear. Just be ready at six," he confirms. "And trust me, you won't be disappointed."

"Wait, what about the fact that co-workers can't date other co-workers," I say, noticing that Ravi is preparing to leave.

He looks at me mischievously. "Well I guess we'll just have to make sure we don't get caught," he responds before closing the door after him.

The next day at work, Ravi actually calls in to say he won't be coming in. I begin to get a bit frantic, thinking that he must've changed his mind about us. I think to call him and tell him that I know exactly what he's up to and maybe even lie and tell him that I've also changed my mind. I always hated being the dumpee. All of these thoughts are running through my mind when I see that he's sent me a text message, saying that we're definitely still on for tonight.

That evening I'm ready early, which is a first throughout my entire dating history. I did not spend hours standing in front of the mirror, trying to decide what to wear. I did not need Teresa to come over and baby talk me into an outfit. And I did not take forever straightening my hair and applying my make up. I figure that this is a time for a fresh new start, so I might as well make the most of it and ditch my old habits.

Ravi arrives at five to six, looking slightly rumpled, yet still cute. He doesn't have roses, or chocolate or any other little gifts for me. It's just him, standing there with a look of excitement on his face. For some reason, this calms me and I take his hand to head out.

"So where are we going?" I ask him, once seated in his car.

"You'll see very soon," he replies with a wink.

During the car ride, we keep up easy conversation. We laugh about the first time we met, I tell him about my recent split from Shawn, and he even admits that although he did like Roz, sometimes he felt like he was settling. Apparently their relationship wasn't as perfect as he'd originally made it out to be. She had no taste for

Indian culture or values, and would even scoff anytime he brought it up. I guess I was right about what a two-faced loser she was from the start. I throw out my plan to give her any sort of makeover or assistance.

We arrive in downtown Toronto, where Ravi immediately parks and finally tells me what the plan is.

"How long have you lived here?" he inquires, once we're standing upon the street.

"My whole life," I reply, intrigued to hear what's coming next.

"Me too," he answers. "But I bet that you've never seen the city like you will tonight."

"What're you talking about?" I ask suspiciously.

"Trust me. Tonight, you're going to see a whole new side of Toronto," he says with a grin.

I can't help but feel my excitement rise. We start to walk down the streets, heading south. I see a couple of bums sitting huddled together in a corner. Ravi stops to drop off some change, but only after making them promise that they will spend it on food.

"Where are we going first?" I take the opportunity to ask him.

"You are so curious," he laughs. "Okay, first I thought that we would take a tour of the Skydome, or now the Rogers Centre since they've renamed it. Then we'll take the elevator up the CN Tower. After, I know this great restaurant that serves the best pasta in the city. And finally, I thought we'd head down the lakeshore and take a walk to burn off some of the calories."

"You mean we're just going to act like a couple of tourists?" I smile.

"Exactly," he nods. "I feel like we live in one of the most exciting cities in the world, and yet none of us ever takes advantage of it. So today I took the day off work to organize all of this. I thought that tonight we'd start with some of the main attractions, and every date afterwards, continue to explore."

"Well, you're very bold, thinking that there will be dates to come," I tease.

He looks at me, suddenly serious. "Jackie, with you, I know that this is just the beginning."

He kisses me then, and it's very sweet and almost innocent. I can feel that he truly means what he's just said. And I can't help but be impressed by what he's offering. No one else has ever suggested such a fabulous first date. I'm more used to the McDonald's and a movie sort of dates. Even Shawn never attempted something so simple and real, and instead tried to charm me with fancy restaurants and trips to Montreal. I should've just known that what I really wanted could be found so easily in the city that's always been my home.

Epilogue:
A Sensible Young Lady

To Do List:
1. Pay bills...wait, already done that
2. Call mom and dad...even though spoke to them last night
3. Clean apartment...again
4. ?????

There is absolutely nothing for me to do. My bills have been paid, my parents are happy with me, my apartment is clean, I have a job, and there is food in the fridge (even though I still haven't learned to cook any of it, but I will). I can't remember the last time that I've felt so relaxed. I've got the whole weekend to myself and for once I don't feel like going out, partying and getting drunk. I'm even caught up on the latest gossip with all of my friends. Christian has decided to take a sculpting class as his first step in re-entering the dating world. He's convinced that sculpting is a real man's sport and is hoping to meet his future partner in the class. Julie is enjoying her single life as always. She's currently in South America with Vince. She's still claiming that it's all in good fun and that she doesn't have any real feelings for him. Nalini managed to talk to her crush Devon without screwing up. I believe they're partnering up to work on an assignment together. Thank God, she doesn't share the exact same genes as me. Teresa finally told her parents that she'd married Luke. She got the most shock value possible, just like she wanted. She told them while they were casually picking out wedding invitations at the store. Her mom dropped the stack she was looking at and almost fainted. They had to call the store clerk to bring a glass of water to revive her and Teresa watched the whole scene with amusement. Her parents got over it fairly quickly and are now thrilled that they don't have to go through the formalities of an actual wedding. They always did seem more laid back to me. Teresa and Luke are now apartment hunting and this time around, I know that Luke is here to stay. I recently got a letter from Mark, apologizing for his behaviour and telling me that he will not be raising the rent and our one year lease is still in effect. This tells me that Shawn has had a word with him, which makes me appreciate him all the more. I feel bad that things couldn't work out between us, but am glad that in the future we will be able to be friends. Sonia is still having her engagement party next weekend. But for once, I don't have any negative feelings towards the occasion. It's not just because I'm with someone right now. I mean, obviously I cannot take Ravi with me, as it'll cause much more shock value than Teresa's situation did. I expect that my parents would probably be so surprised and ecstatic that they would suggest a double wedding, something that Ravi and I obviously have not even thought to discuss just yet. I mean we have only been together for a couple of weeks! Then again, the look on Sonia's face if my parents suggested that she share her special day with me might just be worth it. I'll put it into the maybe pile.

I can't help but think back to the dreaded day when I ruined my clothes, because it was a turning point in my life. Seeing those three little words that read 'dry clean only' scared me more than anything else in my life. They made me realise that in real life people mess up, make mistakes, learn from them and move on. It's almost as if I was too delicate and needed to step out of my fantasy world in order to become more durable, and at the risk of sounding cheesy, machine washable. I can't help but feel that this time around, things really are right, and by right I don't necessarily mean perfect. The thought of what will happen tomorrow doesn't scare me for once. I actually feel as if my life has a purpose and am so proud of myself for accomplishing so much in such a short amount of time. I can't wait to see what else the future (and karma) will throw my way. And like Ravi said to me on our first official date: this is just the beginning.

Hindi-English Dictionary

1. Beta: child, used to show affection
2. Samosa: an Indian appetizer consisting of a fried crust stuffed with potatoes, peas and spices
3. Hindu: one of the religions in India
4. Mandir : place of worship for Hindus
5. Prasad: blessed food served at the Mandir
6. Bollywood: The Indian movie industry, comparable to Hollywood
7. Chai: tea
8. Bindi: decorative dot placed on forehead
9. Pooja: worship
10. Gulaab Jaman: sweet deep fried snack covered in a thick syrup
11. Chee: term used to describe disgust

About the Author

Suzanne is a journalism graduate and currently resides with her parents and sisters, who luckily haven't given her the boot quite yet. She finds shopping with her girlfriends therapeutic, and thoroughly enjoys all of her family get-togethers, as wacky as they may be! Suzanne is passionate about writing and admires people with imagination and the ability to transform their thoughts onto paper. Her life is like a novel filled with comedy, love, mystery and action…but that's a whole different story.

Printed in the United States
110039LV00001B/13-15/P

9 781434 348357